THE WRONG MOVE

And Other Stories

Susan Bass Marcus

ISBN: 978-1-7321434-2-5

Book design by Sarah E. Holroyd
(https://sleepingcatbooks.com)

Cover design by Juliann Whicker, Ginger Dragon Designs

I dedicate this work to Stephen.
You would not be reading this book
without his support and willingness
to read and read and read my stories.

CONTENTS

ACKNOWLEDGEMENTS

THANK YOU TO FRIENDS who have supported and encouraged me to produce this anthology: Stephen, Vicky, Brian, Judith, and Jan as well as my writing group at the Union League Club of Chicago. My gratitude to my editor, Sarah Holroyd and my cover artist, Juliann Whicker for their second collaboration with me on bringing this book to life.

ARBOR VITAE

(PUBLISHED ONLINE AT DARK FIRE, http://darkfire. epizy.com 2015)
In this tale, the tree of life goes on and on.

ar·bor vi·tae, *noun*
1. a North American and eastern Asian evergreen coniferous tree of the cypress family.
2. the treelike form of white matter in a vertical section of the cerebellum.

I LOCKED THE WHEELS of my Aunt Clarice's wheelchair by the front room window and looked across the yard to a line of trees leading to the road on the far side of the property. I could see thick low branches of live oaks my great-grandfather planted long before I was born. I was thinking that another tree wouldn't take well between them now. He had set them too close together. Not that we needed another tree. The oaks provided plenty of shade, but not much room or light for another planting.

Spring was coming; I could see new leaves swelling. With warmer weather, the oaks would drop last year's leaves. Brown and blotched, they would litter the yard. My aunt's arms and face were covered with brown blotches, too.

I was worrying about Clarice and what I was going to do about her. While standing at the window, I checked to see if she was awake and looking at the oaks, too, but her eyes were still closed. Her head tilted to the right and her lower lip sagged with the tilt. I dabbed away a thin line of drool with an old soft diaper and tucked my new pink mohair throw around her bony shoulders. I didn't want her to catch a chill. Every so often, she *heh-heh*'ed a sharp intake of breath and didn't let it go for a minute or so, but she didn't cry or groan. The good side of her mouth curved in a smile.

A few days ago, her eyes were wide open while she watched my face as I spoon-fed her some protein drink. She smiled at me and gurgled a little laugh. The rest of the day she slept, struggled awake to breathe, then dozed again. If she felt hunger pangs, her motionless body rooted to that chair didn't show it.

When I worry, I do chores. After scanning the yard and the oaks, I filled the sink and scrubbed the casserole dish I'd left to soak overnight. I started to imagine myself, helpless like Clarice. Would I end up like her, a dead weight barely able to lick a spoonful of soup? I watched the soapy water swirl down the drain.

Someone was at the door. Through the window, I could see Jason's red Toyota pickup. A monster truck. How does he drive that thing? My feet wouldn't reach the pedals. Jason always teases me whenever I point out that a smaller truck would do just as well. "This is a guy's truck. It works for me," he snorts and laughs, then ends with a bout of coughing. He smokes, a lot. When his work has him lifting heavy bundles, he wheezes.

"Hey. Come in," I said and pointed to Clarice by the window. "She ate yesterday morning but hasn't moved since then. Sleeping like a log."

He laughed. "Like a log. I figured." He coughed and cleared his throat.

"I'm worried about her. The way she's not moving, only breathing in bits, and, well, smiling, in her way."

"I can see she's wilting fast. Have you thought about where you'd like to place her?"

I did not answer right then, not wanting to think about it. I'd worried more about my own self lately, not having anyone to care for me when my winter came. I smiled to myself at the thought of leaves falling off my fingertips.

"What're you grinning at, Sharon? Best move her now while her heart's still beating."

A shiver ran through me. It was happening so quickly. That branched part of Clarice's brain that kept her going—the cerebellum?—had dropped its leaves in a way, but no new buds were sprouting to quicken her. I sighed and didn't say anything for a while. Jason sat on the sofa. He rested his elbows on his knees and peeled off his work gloves.

"Jason, where will we take her?"

"I thought you talked about that place near Beaufort?"

"Where Ronnie is? No, that's too far away. I'd like a place just outside the village, with plenty of ground cover, some water nearby."

He said, "Like those live oaks over there. Without them, this summer'd cook you through and through."

"You know the story of those oaks, about my great-granddaddy? They come from good people, very generous. They keep on giving, don't they, with that shade and all, and places to sit and read a book?"

Jason massaged his stiff hands, then with a quick nod took the mug of hot coffee I offered him. The old sofa sagged as he settled back into it. He stretched out his long legs. His free hand scratched his short greying beard. "Like the old apple trees?"

"Like the apple trees, except I didn't sit in them to read."

"Just hated cutting them down when they sickened."

"But I'll always have the pips."

"Well, now, as for—"

But I interrupted him: "I was thinking that we could move her to a spot by the fairgrounds. She loves—used to love—the noise and the funnel cakes. They should be happy to have her there. Adam says there's plenty of room. They could plant at least ten trees along that road going to the pens."

"I'll have to talk to him, then. It'll take me a while to get there, to look at this place you're talking about. What's it called?"

"I think they call it *Quiet Acres* or is it *Plenty Acres*? Well, it's *Acres*-Something."

The right side of Jason's mouth lifted to signal a weak smile. "Stop worrying about Clarice; it will all be fine, especially now with this good weather."

"I'm going with you," I said and pressed my lips together to keep them from quivering.

Jason stood up and walked to the sink. He rinsed the mug and left it there, then walked over to Clarice and squatted in front of her. He tapped her hand and waited to see if she'd move, but my aunt didn't respond. He pulled on his yellowing leather gloves and shrugged. "Nothing. So, you mean you'll come later when we move her?"

I nodded. "Of course. What'd you think I'd do, wash my hands of her?"

"No, never said that. Whatever suits you. I'll be back after I see Adam. Just to be sure. And he can help with the move."

"'Bye then."

"See you later today. You okay?"

"Right as rain."

Jason closed the door and I heard the truck grind. He'd left it in gear again. Must have been in a hurry. I wasn't. Clarice sat there, facing the window where

I'd left her, but I didn't hear any of her usual gurgling breaths. I wiped away a long string of spittle from her chin then held her wrinkled, cool face in my hands. The wrinkles ran like oak bark from the outer corner of each eye to her chin.

I held my ear near her mouth. Wheezing. She was wheezing. Was that fluid in her lungs? No, not in her lungs, but in her throat and just below. A death rattle, they called it? She wasn't swallowing anymore. Her bird cage of a chest was rising and falling like a gorgeous murmuration of starlings.

Clarice wasn't gorgeous, never was, actually; but I remember her as pretty, dressed up for special occasions, when we all were younger and the family had gathered. Now, her short white patches of hair barely covered her darkening scalp. She had enjoyed her 100th birthday party, especially the chocolate cake and ice cream. Really high grade ice cream. Nothing but the best. She had stayed awake for two hours and kept turning her fuzzy head to look at all of us.

I took a pencil to her eyebrows, so sparse. Only a few grey wisps dotted the bone above her eye sockets. Her lips, nearly the same rusty color as her cheeks, hung open. Her earlobes hung, too, stretched from years of wearing heavy pendant earrings. Her withered arms, like knotted dry branches, lay across her lap.

I thought, Jason's right. Time to move her.

All the things we needed for the move were in the back shed. My work gloves, simple thick brown cloth ones, lay on a shelf in the mud room. No little shoes tracked mud in here anymore. Ronnie's neither. I slipped on a light jacket and the gloves. That grey day pressed down on me, but I unlocked the shed and heaved some supplies into an old, steel framed laundry basket sitting on the four-wheeled cart I use for hauling. I struggled to push it across the yard and into the kitchen. Leaving it by my table, I went back to the shed to lock the door.

A bushel basket half-full of apples sat just inside the shed door. I'd forgotten about them. I gathered a half dozen or more in my apron and carried them into the kitchen. After cleaning, peeling, and coring them, I sliced the apples into a saucepan with some butter and sugar. When they started to boil, I lowered the flame and let them simmer.

An hour later, the applesauce was cool enough. I spooned some into a little Pyrex bowl and mixed in a few of the prepared pips stored months ago. I remember thinking this has to work. I used a little stainless souvenir spoon from the Twin Cities to coax some of the sauce onto Clarice's tongue. She swallowed, coughed, and swallowed some more, until she had eaten it all. She didn't move otherwise, didn't open her eyes.

Satisfied, I pushed the steel basket into the living room, right up to the side of Clarice's wheel chair. This wasn't going to be easy, for me alone. Shrunken as she was, she was still a dead weight. A welcome sound interrupted my worries. Jason's truck.

I looked out and saw Adam was with him. A good sign.

They came around back to the kitchen door, which I'd left ajar. Jason took in a deep breath. "Applesauce?"

I nodded.

He said, "Always makes me think of cooler weather."

"Well, it's spring now and this was the best way to get her to eat."

"Did she swallow any pips?"

I nodded again. "We were talking about giving back, so I thought, you know…"

Adam shifted uneasily and pushed back the bill of his trucker's cap. Blinking his close-set dark eyes, he said, "By the fairgrounds, we need shade trees, not fruiters."

With a wave of his big hand, Jason shooed away Adam's objection. "We'll plant it far from the fence, the farthest, in fact."

"And leave room for others."

"Will do. So, what have you got there?" Jason rummaged in the laundry basket and yanked at the end of the bolt lying at the bottom. "Is this natural burlap or that factory crap? You know only the natural stuff decays."

"It's natural." I paused and took a deep breath. "Do you have some mycorrhiza, that fungus in your truck? The roots won't take without it."

"Got it. Mulch, too."

Adam hitched up his jeans. "C'mon, let's get going. I've got a delivery coming to the grounds."

I pushed the basket next to Clarice so we wouldn't have to go far for the supplies. By pressing a lever, I lowered her wheelchair back slowly until she lay flat. Jason raised the foot rest and I passed the box cutter to him. He pulled a length of the burlap and lay it along Clarice's legs until he was satisfied that he had enough. I hadn't noticed the small sack he had carried into my kitchen. I could see the label: Tru-Gro Slow-Acting Fertilizer. He scooped up a cupful.

He said, "Pour that around her ankles while we wrap them." Her legs had been crossed for a long time now and it was hard to see where one ankle began and the other left off.

Jason poked at them and said we'd have to separate them or one would strangle the other. He handed me one end of cloth. We tucked some between her ankle bones and wound another length around her legs. I was glad Jason was there; otherwise I would have had a hard time.

Before pushing her chair down to the truck, Adam slit the wrapping along the sides of Clarice's legs. He left the bit around her ankles closed. Jason hopped onto the flatbed and helped Adam hoist the chair up a ramp, then he secured it with bungee cords to metal hooks bolted to the floor.

"You said you're coming with us, so sit up front," Jason pointed to the truck's passenger side. "Adam will ride back here." Adam sat himself on a folded tarp next to the wheelchair's legs. Jason pulled the ramp up, jumped to the ground, secured the tail gate, and slid into the driver's seat.

The ride to the fairgrounds took about a half hour. Once we left my place, nothing much along the state road caught my eye except a mix of saplings and young trees starting about 10 yards or so to the side of the Sibley house, far from a stand of much older, bigger trees. The big family that bought the place from the Sibleys moved in just about 30 years ago. So many new trees on their property. The rest of the way we passed rolling fields all cleared, tilled, and mostly planted.

Jason turned off SR12 onto CR44 that led to the fairgrounds. The field usually used for parking was nearly empty. Gusts blowing across it raised little dirt devils. My insides felt like they were whirling through me, too, emptying out as I was. Clarice hadn't spoken to me or anyone else in so long. I missed her chatter, her songs, even her nutty dancing by the window in the front room. I remember her peasant blouse and a yellow and black skirt made from an African print that swished around her long legs. She'd always been the lively one, from the time I came to live with her. She never had kids. Just me.

An aunt and uncle who lived in the next county raised me. It's only when I was old enough for high school that they sent me to live with Clarice. I've lived here ever since. Married my Ronnie in this house. Last time I visited their orchard, my cousins weren't home. The fruit had already fallen from their trees. I picked up a pear that hadn't rotted yet and bit into it. Juice ran down my chin. The sweet smell and soft fruit reminded me of that aunt. It felt good to be close to her again. I had no idea when those pear trees had been planted; they weren't growing there, of course, when I was living in that house.

Those pear trees also reminded me of the first day I saw their farm. I came to live with my aunt and uncle when I was a girl after my parents disappeared in a freak flood. Half the county was out looking for them. I remember climbing high up into an oak and watching the house just float away. My uncle found their bodies and some of their stuff, like my mother's bracelet, after a long, long search. Too far gone for planting. He had the remains cremated and mixed their ashes with mulch for his trees. I was an orphan.

Our family settled here in 1840. They added to their original parcel by buying all the land between them and the river. With every generation, new plantings added to the trees bordering their open fields. Very pretty from spring through fall. Honestly skeletal during the chill of winter, except for the southern live oaks. Which is why they're called "live" because they don't shed their leaves in the fall like other trees.

Clarice was my father's sister. She'd tried living in the city, but came back to the property and rebuilt a house where our home used to be before the flood. The live oaks were still there. She added other hardwood trees and planted an orchard, like almost everyone else who lives in the county. By the time I moved to her place, the house looked like it had always been there, except it hadn't.

Jason parked the truck. We met at the tailgate. Adam tossed the tarp and some tools to the ground. After the two men slid Clarice's wheelchair down the makeshift ramp, they loaded my arms with the tarp and tools. Jason unbuckled Clarice from the chair. He and Adam slid their arms under her body and slung her over Jason's sturdy shoulder. I carried the gear and walked behind them as they headed around the empty livestock enclosure and over the grassy yard.

Adam pointed to the spot he'd picked out. He took the tarp and laid it out next to the spot. Together the men gently lay Clarice on the opposite side of the spot and began to dig a hole with sloping sides. The dirt they dug out fell in damp clumps on the tarp.

When the hole was as deep as Clarice's legs were long, they lifted my aunt and placed her foot-first in the hole. Jason had to cut away some of the burlap so her roots could spread out. Adam broke up the clumps of soil on the tarp, mixed in some Tru-Gro, then shoveled soil into the hole. Jason wheeled out a water barrel and wet the soil when the hole was half filled, to be sure she wouldn't sink. She was stable, so the men added the rest of the soil to the hole and watered it some more after forming a ridge of soil just beyond the edge of the hole. They watered slowly.

The late day sun broke through the clouds and warmed our heads. Clarice's ears were turning green. Her hair gave off the sweet smell of apple blossoms. We covered her with tree wrap up to her neck to protect her tender new bark from rodents and sun damage.

I asked Jason for the shovel he held. I used it to spread a couple of inches of mulch in a big circle around Clarice, to discourage weeds and hold in the moisture. Lastly, we secured a cage around her exposed parts to protect her from coyotes and other critters. Then we cleaned up the area and took the tools and tarp back to the truck. Jason offered to drive me home, but I couldn't leave just then.

I said, "Come back for me after sundown, okay? I want to be with her for a little while longer."

"Sure. And also maybe tomorrow afternoon? You'll see how she's growing."

"Yes, I'd like to see that. Thanks."

"'Well, 'bye, then."

"'Bye."

I sat cross-legged on the grass next to her planting bed for quite a while. Just as the sun neared the horizon, I noticed Clarice's hair lifting in the breeze. Little strands separated from her scalp and drifted through the wires of the cage. I watched them sail away, past the fairgrounds and out of sight. Eventually, Clarice was bald. Her blotchy skin, once so pink and smooth, was tightening into overlapping plates of bark. I hoped she was happy.

I could see the dust of Jason's truck coming back for me. I poked a few apple pips down under the ring of mulch, just to give her some company, and I stood up. "'Bye, dear Clarice. See you soon," I said as I turned and walked down the road to meet Jason. "'Bye, and good growing."

JUST A NOTE BEFORE I GO

(published in "Masques," Medusa's Laugh Press 2016)

Dr. Joanne Hindlestam is about to go on the journey of her life—to Mars. This tale is a series of letters to her mother.

Tuesday, September 16, 2030

Dear Mom,

We haven't talked much lately, with me living in Houston and you up there in Chicago. You know it's because I've been going through intensive training. You probably tore open this envelope when my letter arrived. I hope you're sitting down as you read this. I could have told you by phone, but this way you'll be holding something of me in your hands—a physical letter and my nail clippings. Seriously, look in the envelope. The clippings have my genomic DNA that you'll have come February, 2031 when I leave Earth as part of the Mars Second Wave backup headed to the Red Planet.

Yes, I am sending you this letter instead of calling, because arguing with me won't change my mind—I've committed to the project—and, besides, you know what arguing does to your blood pressure. As a doctor, I can assure you that, thanks to the break-throughs we've made in geriatrics and tissue regeneration, you will probably outlive me! Not that I plan on dying any time soon.

Life on Mars has not been easy for the first three teams, but they did establish camps. They had a lot of problems, however, with the bio-insertion projects needed for permanent settlements and successful colonization. I understand that they have resolved many of those problems or are close to solutions. I, myself, expect many challenges, but you shouldn't worry. As part of the medical team on Earth that worked on minimizing the risks of space radiation, optic nerve damage, and dementia, I feel especially hopeful that my own expertise in neurology and neuro surgery will complement and add to the care of colonists and the research going on there. Just look at the results of our work here at home. Anyway, you're just one of thousands who have benefitted from Mars Colony Project research. Bet you don't even remember your glaucoma, right?

Here's the hard part: I won't be coming back to Earth. Save those nail clippings, Mom. More are in the DNA data and species bank, along with other samples of my tissues and biome organisms, but those clippings are yours, a sort of Joanne back-up.

I can imagine you saying *why can't my daughter come home for a visit?* It's hard for the layman to imagine but I might bring back possibly devastating alien microorganisms in my human biome if I returned without sterilizing them. You couldn't very well sterilize them, however, without killing me.

I will stay in one of the cave shelter complexes, known as Panda Bear, located near the volcano Arsia Mons, which houses the medical treatment and OR center where I'll be working. No, Mom, the volcano is not active and the caves do shelter colonists from radiation and micrometeoroids. Engineers have been working on exploiting nearby sources of geothermal energy, so you see, I'll be enjoying nearly all the comforts of home: fresh food, warmth, and clean, filtered air. I'll just be missing *you*.

Love, Joanne

∾

December, 2030

Dear Mom,

Two months left. I can't believe how fast time is going. I'll be even busier on Mars. No, I won't be so busy that I'll forget all about you, and Jon, and the cousins. Jon—my twin, my opposite in every way. Can't believe he's still writing those fantasy novels, when life on Earth needs everyone's attention and hard work just to sustain us all. Anyway, I'll have your images with me always, whenever I want to project them on my helmet vidscreen, on the ceiling of my biodome chamber, or on any of our MarSatellite devices.

My right leg has been bothering me. I think I pulled a muscle during training exercises. It's nothing to worry about.

When I can get a comm slot up there, we'll be able to chat, just like on the phone. Really! We'll need to be patient. Our messages will transmit every three to 22 minutes, then you'll see me, your daughter on Mars up front and personal. So, don't worry, we'll keep in touch.

Love, Joanne

~

January 2031

Hi, Mom.

In your last letter, you said you felt like crying all the time. I find that hard to understand. It's not as if we've been living near each other for the past decade. Now I'll just be living, well, farther from you, but I won't be gone as in mute, incommunicado, whatever. We've had our differences but you know that the chance to work on Mars doesn't happen every day. Think of the medical history I'll be making. You should be proud of the work I'm doing.

If I could touch you with this letter, feel your fingers holding it, if I could look right now into your eyes, you would understand how exciting this mission will be—*is!*—for me. I'm working with people who have great expertise—doers, team players, innovators. And after I leave Earth, don't forget you'll still have all the people who've been around you since I first left home: Jon, the cousins, all your friends. We'll talk before the February flight. Till then,

Love, Joanne

~

February, 2031

Dearest Mom, thank you for all your good wishes. I know my news last September took a lot out of you. Jon has been calling regularly and says that you're sick with worry. Let me reassure you. As for the Mars Colony Project, I couldn't be working with more organized, safety-conscious, and upbeat people. That little ache in my leg is nothing. I'm fine.

You asked about the ship. It's so cleverly designed. We know our equipment inside-out (I'm sure I talk about it in my sleep!) and the plans are in my DNA now—joking. I'll be thinking of you and will send a message as soon as I've reached the Arsia Mons.

Love and big hugs,
Joanne

∼

September 16, 2031

ComSatellite Data Transmission
Mrs. Hindlestam,

The Mars Colony Project regrets to inform you that upon her arrival at the Arsia Mons biodome complex, your daughter Dr. Joanne Hindlestam died before she could be safely transported to the medical facility. Cause of death was a pulmonary embolism. A small air bubble traveled to her lungs and fatally blocked a pulmonary artery. Her remains will stay on Mars, in a vacuum pack safely stored in the biodome until they can be sterilized for return to Earth. We thank you for your outstanding daughter's brief but significant service to the Mars Colony Project. Her biodata are stored in our Earth-based system, which, indeed, we can send to you forthwith. We will remit the balance of her stipend along with her remains at the first practical opportunity. In the meantime, you have been named beneficiary of her life insurance policy.

Sending our deepest sympathy,

Miles Elon, PhD, LL. B, M.D.
Project Director

PIECES OF STARS

(published by *after hours*, a journal of Chicago writing and art, Summer 2016)
A woman's journey, swimming to the stars

THE SOUND OF HER flip-flops scuffing the floor brings me back. "Franny," she jollies me, "Franny, wake up. Chocolate pudding!" I hear the smile in her voice and my eyelids flutter open. Her brown eyes are close to mine and I can smell sour rice on her breath. I turn away my head, a body part that still moves. It's Lee; her name is Lee. When she puts hearing aids in my ears, her words reach me clearly. If she forgets to do that, an acrid but not wholly unpleasant whiff of vinegar and spoiled fruit announces her proximity.

Other senses are failing, but I don't care, really. I don't need to touch, to feel things. My left hand is clenched and numb; I can't hold a book. Sometimes I can touch my face or push away a spoon if I don't over-think it. Can't stand the noise and flickering of the old television that Lee wants me to watch with her. Actually, I'm not interested in looking at much in this little apartment—except maybe my son. He's nice. Reads me stories and shops for us.

My world used to be so big-city. From my downtown condo, I used to walk everywhere, go out to eat with my friends. They loved to meet me for lunch. I'd have a salad in an upscale Italian place right on Michigan Avenue, joke with the waiter, munch and chat about friends who weren't there, husbands who had left or passed away. Then one of my friends suddenly died in a car crash. Months later, another one's lung cancer killed her, and soon after that, I had a couple of strokes. I remember the first one, the second—not so well.

"Here, taste this pudding, Franny. Your son bought it for you. It's so-o-o good. Yum-yum." Lee tickles my lips and my mouth gapes open. A glob sits on my tongue. A little gluey. What's the point? She says, "It's full a pro-tee-in, build your muscle. Here, more?" Lee rubs the spoon on my tongue. I gag and close my eyes. My hand quivers to bat the spoon. Lee hovers over me until I hold my breath—I feel her body heat in the space between us. She lets the spoon clatter into the sink and she sighs.

"Okay, Franny. You rest a little. I wash up." I hear her rinsing the container and spoon. The scrape of a pan on the little two-burner stove signals she's making a snack for herself. Probably warming up the rice that's been sitting there since she put me in the wheel-chair this morning and, groaning softly, pushed me into what the management calls a living room. I sit there all day, hardly living. My scenery changes when someone wheels me outside and around the parking lot—for fresh air, they tell me. Lee says it's snowing today. No field trips.

Lee doesn't wheel me downstairs to meals any-more. She complained to my son when he last visited that the manager barred us from the dining room and the lounge. Someone made a fuss because Lee was sitting at the table to feed me. That someone didn't want to sit with me anymore. Said I slobbered. I think people don't want to share their table with my nurse.

This place is supposed to be "assisted living," which means they help you a little, but they don't allow actual live-in nursing. I moved here ten years ago because my son was worried about my living alone downtown after recovering really well from my first stroke. I let him install me here. In a couple of months, management started "assisting" me all the time: "Franny, sit here, Do this activity. Go to the gym. Get your hair done." Who asked them?

When I first moved to this place, people used to re-quest my table. "Why can't you sit me with Franny?" they'd complain. "She's so smart. Such good conver-sations." Not now. I guess they feel depressed around me. The kitchen sends up a tray. Lee eats my leftovers, whatever she didn't put in the blender for me.

My appetite's gone, too. My tongue gets in the way of chewing. Lee asks me too many questions. To escape her, I let my eyelids fall, the way they used to at Symphony. Sometimes, during a concert when they felt scratchy and dry. I would let my eyes drift shut. I would feel as if a gray, music-punctuated cloud wrapped me in warm mist. Not for too long. My head would snap back, and I'd wake up again for the rest of the program.

Now, whenever I close my eyes, I feel little bits of whatever is me fly away. They peel off and separate from me. No pain—like my arm shedding dead skin cells. That's how it goes. A kind of sloughing. Sometimes I follow the bits into the dark spaces behind my closed lids. The first time I floated after them, like a lazy swimmer in a deeply shaded pool, I felt lost. What was I doing there, alone and away from my caregiver, my over-attender? An escaping strand of my hair would bob in front of where my nose should have been. In the dark it shone like a silvery thread and wriggled away until it broke apart into countless little twinkling dots.

Always, out there in the dark, the wheelchair disappears. My arms stretch wide and my fingers flex. My legs and toes kick and wriggle. I swim and pull myself forward with breaststrokes and frog kicks, head up to keep my hair dry, into a sea of silvery, sparkling pinpoints. Each stroke makes me laugh. I remember how to swim with strong strokes, not like the one that took my words and froze my body.

I keep on swimming until a whining sound dissolves the sea around me and I feel my body grow heavy and stiff.

"Time to change your diaper, Franny. Sorry, sorry, but you know, dear . . . after you eat, you poop." Lee is very tall and she has heavy, flabby arms. She lifts me like I'm a watermelon. She lays me out on the bed and apologizes as she cleans me up, always with the same clucking sounds. I'm just glad to be rid of the itch. She washes my bottom and dabs ointment into skin folds. I don't feel the pressure of her fingers on my right leg and arm, but I do glimpse her hands moving around my numb side. Some days I can see better, but not today. My eyes are tired of staying open.

"Don't want you having that rash, dear. I get in trouble with you-know-who," Lee tells me that to day the hospice nurse is coming. She diapers me with extra pads and dresses me in slacks with an elastic waistband, a tee-shirt, and my favorite loose white blouse with long sleeves. She slips socks on my feet—I don't walk in this all too solid place. Pairs of shoes used to cover my closet floor. I wonder if some-one took them.

My son hired Lee after my last stroke. It left me so weak that I couldn't dress or feed myself anymore, couldn't even use a walker. Because a doctor said it looked like I'd be dead in six months, insurance covered hospice care for me at home. I didn't die. The in-surance stopped covering hospice care and Lee and my son did their best, I guess. Lee said he was paying for my diapers and ointments.

They put me in hospice care again. A nurse visits three times a week, although I'm not keeping track. A doctor sees me, too. Everyone talks to me in a chirpy, cheery voice: "Hi, there, Franny. You look so pretty today!" or "So nice to see you. Beautiful weather isn't it?" I haven't been outside. Wouldn't know. Every day feels the same; only the aches and spasms change and stab at different parts of my body.

I'm eighty-nine and still alive, still *amazing*. "You're amazing, Mom"—what my son tells me. Eighty-nine years old. Time flies. Wasn't I just seventy and having lunch with my friends? So they started hospice care again, sure of my mortality this time around. Anyway, I can't tell them what I'm thinking, that I don't care. My son says he can't understand my words but knows what I'm thinking. How can he know what I'm thinking? He wears me out with his talking.

Lee coaxes me to take my pills in some chocolate creamy thing she makes in the blender. To refuse it, I grunt a kind of 'no' and press my lips together. She knows I'm not going to sip any of it, but she tries again and again until I close my eyes and start to cough. Then she stops; she'll lie to the nurse, I suppose.

The hospice nurse also told her to give me some drops to help me breathe. She squeezes them onto my tongue and I don't give her any trouble. Lee says she doesn't like me to be so doped up because then I don't eat and she so wants me to eat. She doesn't give me as much morphine as Nurse wants her to.

Just as well. The morphine sends me into some kind of a fog and I can't remember where I've been; but I also don't feel so angry and sad when I swallow the drops; but my truly good times happen without the drops, in the dark place behind my closed eyes. If I could just get Lee to put me back in bed now, I could leave again, follow my bits and pieces into that dark place. Enough sitting in this wheelchair. It numbs my behind. My legs feel like logs.

When my son visits and pats my left foot to wake me up, I hardly feel his hand. Hoping to get a smile out of me, he tells me stories about places he has been and the people he's met. Very sweet, so I smile. Sometimes I even laugh, but can't stop myself. He thinks I'm laughing at his story, but it's just some kind of brain fart. A little drool seeps out of the corner of my mouth. He wipes my chin and goes on talking. After I've given him enough attention, I close my eyes and follow my ship-jumping body pieces to my other place. Lee says he is coming tomorrow and we'll do all this again.

Before Nurse leaves, she helps Lee put me back in bed. She raises the mattress behind my back and tells Lee to keep it up. My head rests on a pillow. They want my chin to be closer to my chest. That way, I can swallow more easily and breathe without choking. They should let me choke, although I don't think I'd like all that gasping and coughing. I saw Nurse whisper to Lee. She forgot to turn her back as she usually does. I could make out she was telling Lee something like, "It won't be long. That kind of breathing, you know."

Time to get out of here. I hate when they talk like that, as if they see only a brittle package wrapped in parchment, left behind like waste. After so much swimming in the dark sea behind my eyelids, more than half of me has drifted into the billowing star clouds anyway. I hear a deep, almost groaning pulse rising and falling between galaxies. Starry wheels surround me and pull me into their core. I feel lighter than ever. A feather of a person. A bird of paradise. A hot-air balloon rising and sailing into a swirling, shimmering cosmic soup. I am racing, plowing through the iridescent waves to reach my escaping tiny bits. Although my arms pull and push through the sea of stars, the sea also flows inside and through me. Nothing separates us, yet I can't catch up with myself. No matter. The deeper I slip into the sea, the calmer I feel.

"What day is it? What is your name?"

Who said that? I open my eyes to painful bright light. Someone is standing next to my bed. I don't know the face. The person bends over me and asks me again, "What is your name?"

I know I'm Franny. Why should I tell him, whoever he is? I let out a groan and hear myself say, "Fuh-fuh" and I smile. That's good enough for government work. Now who used to say that? I can't remember.

So many things I can't remember—faces, names of things, what I'm doing here in this bed.

A tube in my nose tickles, but I can't raise a hand to pull it out. My mouth purses and opens like a fish sucking water for its gills, but I can't catch enough air. Little star bits fall like snow in the dark and I float away until glittering waves pick me up and carry me out to sea. When we swam in the Dead Sea, I floated like this, but my own dark sea is tossing me around. I'm thrusting my arms and legs with my breast-strokes. Pull-kick-pull-kick. I am aiming for a very large star that looks warm and friendly, an orange crayon sun that sits in the upper left-hand corner of my son's drawing. A sunny day, a forever of sunny days.

～

The thin, gray-haired man assumed his mother had not recognized him before she lost consciousness, but when he kissed her dry forehead, she opened her eyes, looked up at him, and opened her mouth. He would always remember the smile that brightened her face.

The nurse checked his mother's pulse and shook her head. She started her usual condolence speech, but stopped when she saw that he had dozed off. She closed the old woman's eyelids with a gentle stroke, and was going to cover her face with a bedsheet after lowering the mattress, but the man suddenly woke up and asked her to stop. He needed to look at her face just a bit longer. The nurse nodded, said, So sorry, Sir," and went into the living room. Now they were waiting for someone official to arrive and confirm his mother's death.

Not long before those last moments, he had closed his own eyes, maybe for a minute, maybe more, and he drifted into what he assumed was a hypnagogic hallucination. It went like this: he and his mother were on the balcony of her condo. It felt so real. They were looking at the Milky Way in the night sky and as they stood there, stars began to tumble toward them. At first they fell slowly and looked like stray, ragged pieces of chrysanthemum fireworks. Very soon, however, they picked up speed and the man was sure they were hurtling directly at him and his mother.

His arms stretched out to push his mother back into the condo, but he was too small to protect her from the giant stars that surrounded them and ignited the iron railings. The old woman fell away from him and became really tiny; and the man began to swim freestyle through all the star matter crashing down on them. He plowed on, flailing and churning through the cosmic particles toward a giant orange star. Before diving into its boiling mass, he woke up. He saw his mother had stopped breathing. His hand had been squeezing hers. As he slowly released his grip, he could see his fingers had pressed dents into her soft flesh. He called to her. He tapped her bony shoulder. He looked up at the nurse. The woman shook her head and said she was sorry, but his mother was gone. Her words passed through him, but the dream of a celestial catastrophe still burned.

After the funeral and the burial, whenever the man closed his eyes to nap or sleep for the night, he would see stars behind his eyelids. Little bits of twinkling light gave him the feeling that minute parts of his own self, maybe his skin shedding dead cells, floated into that star-scape and, receding from his view, absorbed enough starlight to form their own constellations. He could swear that, sometimes, they rearranged themselves and he would see something resembling his mother's face in their glow.

The Wrong Move

A dark fantasy with supernatural menace

L ATER, MUCH LATER, I regretted signing the lease. Not because of the dog. I like other people's dogs when they are on a leash, like the good dog that once lived downstairs. But when a loose dog with no master approaches me on the street, I always sweat with fear.

My friends warned me, "Ella, don't sign yet. Look at some other properties." But I couldn't resist the apartment's location—close to a park, a short walk to an upscale supermarket, and three blocks from bistros and bookstores. I needed the change.

When I saw the listing for a two-bedroom walk-up with a balcony, vintage 1950s, I called the agent and met her at the address on Cedargrove Street a few hours later. We climbed a tidy, carpeted staircase to the second floor where I saw the landing was shared by just two units.

"Mrs. Volkman, the same owner rents both units," the agent said as she noticed me staring at the other unit's gouged door bottom. She pulled her ponytail, adjusted her flower-patterned scrunchie, and pointed to the scratches. "The company will fix that. Anyway, I've never heard of any complaints about that unit next door." She unlocked 2B. "I think you'll like this one."

From the apartment's short entrance hall, we walked into a wide, sunny space the agent called a "living/dining combo" where she pointed out tall windows that faced a street lined with mature trees. The kitchen, with French doors leading to the balcony and plenty of cabinets and newer appliances, made me giddy. It was tucked into the far corner of the main room but was as bright as the rest of the space. Several LED fixtures along the ceiling and over the counters added to the light pouring in from the windows. I loved the tile floor that extended in a wide arc out of the kitchen and into the area suitable for a small dining table. How easy to keep clean!

A master bedroom with a bathroom plus another bathroom off the second smaller bedroom was quite an improvement over the place I was currently renting. My tiny one-bedroom at the end of a gloomy corridor on the 24th floor of a high-rise near the expressway had never felt like home. Only the bus stop outside the high-rise's front door compensated for my feeling of being isolated in a giant beehive. With just a little time left on my lease, I'd started looking for a cozier place.

"You said both units on this floor belong to the same owner?" I asked the agent.

"Yes, and that's a one-bedroom but I don't know

who lives there now. The owner wants twelve hundred a month for this one. People sometimes share a unit if that's too much."

"No, I can manage. I'd like to take this one if the condo association approves, since it matches my wish list. Why did the last renter leave? Or did the owner live here?"

"It's not a condo, but four units, all rentals. About the owner, I understand a title-holding land trust owns it. I'm sorry but I can't share information about the last occupant, even if I knew. So, tell me, now that you've had a look, shall we discuss the lease? You know the terms, besides the rent?"

She ran through a list of fees, limits, repairs, restrictions—you name it. I couldn't remember a quarter of what she said. I assumed they'd be explicit in the lease and my lawyer would take care of it all, as he did the last time I moved.

"Great," the agent said when I mentioned my lawyer. "I'll send him the papers. When can you meet to sign the lease?"

We agreed on the date. A few weeks later, a glum, emaciated man in a dull gray suit showed up to represent the land trust. My lawyer accompanied me and kept whispering I should not sign a two-year lease. "What if you hate the place?" he said. "Something could go wrong, and you'd be stuck. They won't let you sublet. I strongly advise you to find a different rental in a better neighborhood."

I signed.

By the first week of October, I was the happy occupant of a cheery and comfortable apartment. My friends' reactions were predictable. "What do you know about the neighborhood? Do you have a doorman? How are you going to get around? Where's the closest bus stop?" I ignored their questions.

I put off telling my son I'd moved again. When the sale of my old house had looked promising and I had started to downsize for a life in the high-rise, Lonnie was 21 and had started working in England. Certain he'd never claim them, I had sold most of his old LP records, piano sheet music, and a few odd paranormal novels—about shapeshifters like werewolves, merpeople, and vampires—to vintage vendors on the North Side. One morning, as I was packing for the move, I emailed Lonnie to let him know I wanted to e-transfer the receipts to his bank. He answered, "Should have asked me first, but keep the money. I'm not playing piano anymore."

I typed, "You never mentioned that stuff in all the years you've been away. I assumed you didn't care. Anyway, I don't have your address. Give it to me so I can send you a few other things."

He didn't answer for a few minutes. "Don't bother sending anything. I'm sorry. You caught me by surprise. I haven't heard from you in so long."

I wrote, "All right, but you never call me either, you know."

"Yeah, well . . ." From then on, his emails were

short and not sweet.

Moving from a three-bedroom suburban ranch home to a high-rise, I had needed to discard a lot of belongings. Long after my husband's death, his clothes still carried signs of his life: stale cigarettes tucked in the pocket of a brown tweed sport coat, the mineral scent of his gray flannel business suits, a yellow cashmere sweater vest bearing hints of his lemony aftershave—ghosts of his days were hanging on one side of the closet. On the opposite rack, my size-eighteen-petite polyester dresses drooped in re-cycled dry-cleaner bags. After my pre-diabetes diag-nosis, I'd dieted down to a size eight, but never got around to ridding myself of my "fat" clothes. I still enjoyed a good meal, including dessert.

Not that the house was too big, but I grew tired of cleaning it. I wasn't getting any younger. Then, there was the commute to work—what a waste of time. Time, the bathroom mirror was saying to me, you can't afford to waste it on the headaches this house gives you. Look at yourself.

I looked, good and hard. My reflection was a thin-ner version of my mother, like her mouth's little sag-ging corners and the small puckers of skin under her eyebrows. My eyeliner always reprinted itself on my puffy eyelids. Time's corrosion was etching tiny lines from my upper lip to my nose. When I stared into the reflection of my eyes, however, still brown and free from capillary entanglements, I saw the origi-nal me, the one I knew was alert to possibilities. A fresh start and an infusion of cash would energize me, I thought. So I sold the house and moved into the high-rise. Now, with even fewer possessions, I relished having a cozy place, more to human scale, and on a peaceful street.

The first week in my new walk-up, I spent hours arranging furniture. I put a daybed in the second bedroom in case Lonnie ever visited me. Delightful dilemmas arose: Should my bed go up against the window or face it? If I angled the bed into a corner, would my old armchair fit? Would a bright Hawaiian-themed shower curtain be too much to face in the morning? Little things. I was so busy setting up the kitchen and finding places to store my still abundant gadgets that I didn't notice anything wrong with the place.

At the start of week two, settled in my armchair with a mug of tea, I was relaxing with a book of short stories. Scratching sounds distracted me from a slow-moving tale about a ghost in a church. I groaned at the possibility of rats and felt my lawyer's warning about signing a two-year lease nag at my conscience. A persistent scrick-scrick was coming from the kitchen, behind the wall I shared with 2A. I put the book down and opened one cabinet after another. No sign of rats or bugs. Everything looked clean. The scratching sound stopped as I slammed the last cabinet door. Maybe they had a curious cat. Our old tomcat used to scratch endlessly on our bedroom door.

Then, I heard a distant howl, like a coyote's. I decided to check the street and, just as I stepped onto my balcony, I heard a whimper, the kind a lonely pet makes. I looked outside and scanned the street, bathed in sunlight. No coyote trotting down the sidewalk. Nobody walking a dog.

Circling around the apartment I realized the whimpering came from somewhere inside the building. When I brought my tea mug back to the kitchen sink, I heard it more clearly. It was coming from the apartment next door. A dog, not a cat, I thought. So, someone does live there. Poor pooch probably misses his fur-parent.

"There, there, boy. They'll be home soon," I said up against the bit of kitchen wall not lined with cabinets. The whimpering stopped. Atta girl, Ella Castle Volkman, there's your good deed for the day.

On Saturday, I thought my neighbors would be home, so I decided to introduce myself. My house keys in hand, I crossed the landing with a small plate of caramel-chocolate-chip bars and knocked on the door. No answer. I knocked again and called out, "Hello?"

As if in response, I heard something shuffle across the floor, coming toward the door.

"Hello," I said again. "It's your neighbor, Ella."

No answer. No one opened the door. Then I heard a thump or two. Assuming the dog was alone while his owners were out to brunch or something, I went back to my place and ate one of the bars myself. Then I tackled the last annoying bits of unpacking I'd put off.

~

Once I'd emptied all the boxes from my move and felt organized, I decided I'd had enough already with carry-out and convenience store food. I grabbed my new shopping cart and headed to the supermarket. I loved that little cart, with its vinyl cover and wheels that glided up stairways. Marino's was a couple of blocks away and on that warm, sunny day, contentment flooded me. I had a lovely new home, a neighborhood full of conveniences, and plenty of time to enjoy my retirement.

I liked the way Marino's was laid out: produce section as you came in, then gourmet cheeses, nuts, and condiments—all the foods I really liked to eat, foods my carnivore family used to treat with contempt. Remembering the sad puppy next door to me, I grabbed a little bag of grain-free dog treats and dropped it on top of the whole grain bread, veggie burgers, nuts, goat cheeses, and vegetables I'd piled up.

With a cart full of ingredients for tasty future meals, I walked back to my building. As I rounded the corner to my block, I saw a man ahead of me. His dog, a knee-high pooch with a curly black coat, kept looking up at him, whether in adoration or puzzlement, I couldn't guess. They turned into my building's walkway, and soon I joined them in the vestibule.

The man looked nice: tightly curled graying hair,

wire-rimmed spectacles, dressed in a barn coat and corduroy trousers. He was fumbling for his keys.

"Hi, don't bother. I have mine out," I said.

He looked up at me as if surprised to find me there. "Oh, well, yes, thanks."

"I'm, Ella Castle. I've just moved into 2B. Are you my neighbor across the landing?"

"No, I live one flight down in 1A. Name's Dave Straybill." He held out his hand and shook my free one holding the key. "Ouch, sorry, didn't mean to squeeze. Are you all right?"

"Of, course. I just thought you might be in 2A because of the dog."

"The dog?"

"Yes, I've heard a dog whimper in 2A, I think, by my kitchen wall."

"That's strange, I'm the only resident here with a dog . . . or do you have one, too?"

I couldn't answer Dave right then. My mind was racing. I knew I'd heard a dog in 2A. I told him so.

"Well . . . Mrs. Castle . . . I can tell you I've never met any other dog in this building. Your neighbors either. Kinda quiet, they're kinda quiet—now." He gazed at his dog, which was pawing his knee. "Okay, King, we're going up. He's hungry, you see."

"Oh, gosh, I'm sorry. Go on. I didn't mean to keep you. 'Bye, King. Here . . ." I rummaged for the treats in my Trolley Dolley. "Here's a yummy munchie for you. Oops, do you mind?"

"No problem," Dave said with a slight dimpled

smile. King gave me a quick, friendly bark, licked my outstretched hand, and scooted away as soon as Dave dropped the leash. As I passed them on the way up to my floor, I waved. Dave wasn't looking in my direction. No matter. The moment I stepped into my unit, I felt calm, relaxed, and thoroughly at home. Cute dog, I thought. Hope I bump into them again.

I slipped off my flats and, dragging my cart behind me, walked across the cool floor to the kitchen. So much easier to pull my purchases straight out of the cart rather than haul paper bags that ripped or plastic bags that sagged and were hard to recycle. I shopped with a clear conscience.

I wanted to sanitize a couple of the lower cabinets to store onions, potatoes, and the like, but I had left the task for later, so, now I sudsed up a sponge and started to wash the base. Since I couldn't see into the cabinet's corners, I used the flashlight I kept handy by the phone to light up the back wall. Someone had patched it recently but left it unpainted. It felt rough and gave a little. That was odd. Everything else in the apartment was in good condition.

I happened to have a roll of marble-grained contact paper. I'd used only a foot or two in my last place to cover the top of an old side table. I eyeballed the area and cut a piece of the paper to fit. It covered the defects perfectly. I sat back on my heels, grinning at my success, then stored a bag of onions and a small net sack of garlic inside. My estranged son would have been surprised at the way I was handling all this.

I sighed. I couldn't put off any longer doing a task I'd been dreading. Shopping was a great distraction, but I had to give Lonnie my new contact information. Not only had I changed my address but also my internet provider. I opened my laptop and started an email. "Dear Lonnie, hope all is well in London. Please don't be upset. I've moved again . . ."

∾

Sometimes, Dave and I would meet by the mailboxes in our vestibule. We'd chat for a while. He said he'd quit a desk job to work from home around the same time I'd left my job as a paralegal to care for my ailing husband. When King was with him—which was almost always—I'd commune with the pooch. Squatting, I would sweet-talk him with pats and scratching around his ears and under his chin. He loved it and he loved the treats I carried with me in a little plastic bag. King and I were best friends before long.

Dave must have decided I was worth knowing better since King liked me. He even started to smile during our conversations. Meeting by chance one day just inside our building, I pressed him on the dog noises from next door.

"Look, Dave, I'm sure I heard a dog . . . it whimpered . . . somewhere in our building. It was eerie. You say it's not King?"

"Nah." He patted King's side. The dog jumped back

as if Dave's touch burned. Maybe Dave wasn't King's best friend after all. "He doesn't cry, usually, but. . . ." He scratched the back of his head and pushed his glasses up his nose. "Well, sometimes—not often, let me tell you—I have to leave King alone for a while. Sometimes a long while. Maybe you heard him then."

"Dave, the sound came from next door, not below."

"Sound travels funny around here. You're probably not hearing things, but there are noises in this building. It's quite old. Been renovated several times. Listen, how about a cup of coffee? I'll make a quick espresso. King will be happy since—" Dave smiled and tilted his head. "Coming?"

"Sure, thanks, if it's no trouble."

"None at all."

Dave's place had the same floor plan as mine, minus the second bedroom and bath. A big oak desk sat squarely in the middle of the "living" part of the main room. Where my kitchen had a butcher block counter, a granite-covered island divided his kitchen from the rest of the room.

Dave dropped his keys on a table by the front door and filled a wide ceramic bowl with dog chow. King held back for a moment, then set to eating noisily. Dave sighed. "I've never heard any of the noises you've mentioned . . ." He paused. "Except—"

"Except what?" Sitting on a stool next to the island I was absorbed in the granite's pretty green and black swirls.

"Except, just before my wife died, a few years ago."

"Oh, I'm so sorry. My husband died a while back, too." My turn to pause. Taking a deep breath I asked, "So you did hear noises in 2A?"

"Well, yeah, once. Clarice—my wife—was in home hospice care. I'll spare you the details, but she was near the end. I wanted her to have peace and quiet, but all through the night before she died, neither the nurse nor I could get any rest because of noise from upstairs. Not that those tenants were ever a problem, but on that night, of all nights, I heard heavy steps pacing back and forth overhead. The hospice nurse heard it, too. Clarice was sedated, but I got agitated, and King began to stare at the ceiling and whine. Really creepy.

"I went upstairs and knocked on the door. No one answered. Deathly quiet. So, I went back home. After about ten minutes the pacing started up again. Clarice's breathing changed. The nurse said to prepare myself. Oh, God; that was awful. Clarice died, and the pacing stopped." Dave clamped his lips shut. Raising his eyebrows, he said, "You said you're a widow?"

I nodded.

"How long? Was he sick?"

"Um, his death was complicated."

Dave tilted his head again and stared at me.

"A bizarre accident. A drowning. They never found his body, just his wallet and clothing." I shivered.

"Never found his body? Where, by the lake?" I

nodded. "Did you say your last name is Castle?" He paused for a minute or two. "I'm sorry. It's hard. I heard of another case like that, a guy named Volkman." He paused, waiting for my reaction.

I was practiced in keeping a poker face. "Two times too often, I'd say."

"Yeah. Well, then, as for 2A, I'm sure everything's fine. I never heard pacing again. Since a land trust owns the place, their rep vetted the tenant. Hey, mind if King and I see you home? I'll put my ear to the door. Maybe I'll catch a whimper."

"Oh, that's not necessary, but . . ." Dave had rushed out the door after King. I put my demitasse in the sink, tossed the paper napkin in his wire waste basket, and, closing the door, followed him up the stairs.

On my landing, King dashed to the threshold of 2A and sniffed it, running from one edge of the door to the other.

"Hey, King, quit it. Leave it alone, you dumb dog."

I didn't understand why Dave yelled at King. "He smells it, whatever's in there."

"Nah, sometimes he gets these notions, chases after a nothing, then he calms down."

"He's looking pretty frantic to me."

Crouching next to his dog, Dave reached out to pet him. King snapped at his hand and Dave fell backwards, breaking his tumble with one hand. He cursed. "King, bad dog!" King splayed his front legs and growled. Dave scrambled to his feet. "I guess he wants us to get away from that door."

I fished the treat bag out of my purse. "Here, this might help. There, there, King, good dog."

Easing a serious case of raised hackles, King turned quiet and docile as I offered him a handful of treats. Dave picked up his leash, and King strained toward the stairs.

"What is it, buddy? Wanna go?"

Dave ran after King down the stairs. King scratched furiously at the vestibule door. Dave patted his head and called up to me. "I'm confused. King never acts this way and I know he's not sick. Why don't you talk to Joe, our handyman—you haven't met him? Okay, I'll talk to him. Maybe he will check it out for you."

"Dave, King didn't like something in 2A and he did not want you anywhere near it." He didn't answer. As he passed through the outer door I called, "Who is this Joe? I've never seen a janitor around here."

He yelled back, "A contract maintenance man. Doesn't have to come in all that often. We take care of most problems ourselves and we haven't had many lately until, well, now."

I stepped back from the banister. "Sure, fine, thanks for the suggestion. He must have a master key or something." I put my ear to the door of 2A. Silence. I returned to my place and double-locked the door.

~

By the end of the week, I began to believe Dave—that our 1950s building with its old boiler and pipes probably made many peculiar noises unfamiliar to a former high-rise dweller. Except, this was October, and the heat wasn't on yet. However, I heard no more whimpers or clawing through my kitchen wall. I forgot about them and put off trying to locate the building's handyman. Other projects occupied my thoughts: restaurant or theater dates with friends, exploring the local branch library, and extending my walks around the neighborhood to get more exercise.

On Monday, as I hurried through my building's small, wood-paneled lobby, I tripped and bumped into an older woman. "Oh, my gosh," I blurted. "I am so sorry. I didn't expect to . . . to meet . . . anyone so . . . uh . . . so—"

The petite person I nearly toppled steadied herself and continued shuffling through envelopes in her hand. She sniffed their edges while peering at them through readers resting on the end of her nose. "Didn't expect someone so short?" she said through a brilliant smile. I guessed from her cloud of frizzy, gray hair and rays of laugh wrinkles around her sky-blue eyes she was at least a decade older than I, but younger than her years.

Embarrassed, I said, "Are you okay? I was in a hurry and didn't expect to meet anyone. It's just my mind was—"

"In another time and place," she stopped my blathering. "Well, hi, I'm Fanny Katzer. And you?"

"Ella Castle.

"Castle. Married?"

"Widowed. You?"

"Never married, although I've had my share of . . . boyfriends, shall we say? Well, nice to meet you, Ella. In 2B?"

"Yes, but how did you—"

"Know? The movers. Bit of a racket. And they left garbage on the stairs. Had to clean it up myself, but that's not your fault. Anyway, you like it here?"

"Yes, I'm happy here. I'm really sorry about the mess. I didn't know. Why didn't Joe help clean it up?"

"Joe?"

"The building's contract maintenance man. Dave Straybill said he comes when needed."

"Straybill said that? He has a dog. I don't like dogs." She hissed between her teeth. "Anyway, good luck trying to find this 'Joe' or the landlord if you *do* need something fixed."

"What do you mean?"

"The landlord is not a person; it's a land trust. I pay my rent and they keep the place in shape. Maybe that Joe guy works for them, but I've never called to fix anything so who knows."

Fanny turned away and let herself into the inner hallway. "See you later. I've got bills to pay." She unlocked the door to 1B. I glimpsed a long, red sofa book-ended by enormous lamps sitting on dark wooden tables. Scattered bright cushions caught my eye before she closed the door with a wave. Her place looked cozy.

Pleased I'd met another neighbor worth knowing better, I zipped up my jacket, tightened my favorite blue scarf with a slipknot, and left the building to take a brisk walk. I hurried along the street lined with maples and honey locusts all turning color. The cool air smelled crisp like the first bite of an apple. Invigorated, I strolled past frame and brick cottages mixed with small apartment buildings like mine. Using my phone, I shot a few pictures. Some houses had plastic slides and strollers parked on shallow front lawns. Other buildings had tidy gardens filled with the last plantings of summer just starting to wither.

When the pace is steady, the sidewalks smooth, and my feet take over the walk, I get to thinking. I wondered why Fanny Katzer said she didn't know Joe the handyman. Dave did and was confident about his helping me. I slapped my forehead: I'd forgotten all about 2A's howls and scratching. I wondered if Fanny had ever heard dog noises upstairs. Not a dog-lover, she would have noticed. I considered inviting her up for coffee. Then I'd ask her about it. But first, we'd talk about anything normal. Then I'd bring up the building and . . . lost in my thoughts, I didn't notice I'd come to a dead end. A sprawling red brick school, dark with nothing in the windows, blocked the intersection. I decided to turn right (I always did that in museums, at the supermarket, hotels, even if I was supposed to go the other way). On that day, I should have turned left.

~

I decided to stretch my walk for another few minutes. One streetlamp at the intersection cast a dim but broad orange light as I rounded the corner. I didn't realize it was so late, nearly 5:30. I tossed my cell phone back into my tote bag and continued my neighborhood stroll. A full moon would be rising soon, and I looked forward to enjoying its light in the chilly evening air. All I needed now was Beethoven's *Moonlight Sonata* playing in the background to perfect the scene. I reached for my phone again and asked Google to find the piece. As I passed the next few small houses my tote muffled the sonata's rising and falling da-da-da, da-da-da, da-da-da and slowed my pace.

I looked around. The buildings on this block were run-down and dark, not like my block's cheery apartments and bungalows. Here no windows welcomed the passerby with warm, amber-tinted curtains or shades; most were boarded up. I passed an aged frame cottage. A dim blue light glowed in its one rear window. Broken steps rose to a sagging front porch—a dreary contrast to the sprightly middle section of the sonata playing in my tote—and heavy curtains hung in the downstairs windows and pulled shades covered those upstairs.

In front, a cracked and littered sidewalk matched the cottage. I kicked a grimy plastic bottle to the curb. Crumpled on the patchy parkway lay a damp, moldy glove. Further on, a torn man's sock, old bones (KFC?), and a few leather coat buttons led me to a lot, empty except for a large, cone-shaped structure at its center—a peeling trash burner.

As the pace of the sonata picked up, I walked the lot's perimeter for a better view. Pulling out my phone and hoping I had enough light, I photographed it just as the sonata was gaining in frenzy. At that moment I heard a low growl.

The streetlights on this block were out, and in the growing dark I saw the shadowy shape of a large dog circling the structure. It approached me in slow, measured steps with hackles raised. A thick thatch of gray and dull white fur covered his brindle coat. My heart quickened with the last agitated bars of the sonata as I felt panic clouding my thoughts. Couldn't run. He'd have charged me; big enough to tear me apart. As he neared, I could see his fangs exposed by a horrendous snarl.

Facing the beast, I began to back up slowly toward the intersection and hoped some other person out for a walk would help me. The sonata ended and Lonnie's favorite, Beethoven's *Piano Concerto No. 2*, followed on the YouTube thread.

While terrified, I swallowed an involuntary laugh as the strains of the "Adagio" wafted out of my hand. My late husband had loved hearing Lon-

nie play it, until he fell ill and lost interest in everything.

The dog stopped moving. I was sure his crouch
signaled an imminent leap at my throat. Stifling his
fierce growl, he lifted his muzzle and howled with
such notes of grief I nearly felt pity for him. Or did
the music hurt his ears? Whatever the reason, he
whined and turned away from me. Circling the cone,
he paused, turned back for a moment, then disappeared inside it.

Not wanting to lose sight of this creature, I continued backing toward the intersection. Once I saw
that the dog had lost interest in me and I was back
on my street, I looked around. No one else was out
walking. Not one person or car was anywhere near. I
hurried home and debated reporting my encounter.
On the loose, the dog might harm kids going to and
from that school. I decided to be a good neighbor
and call Animal Control.

~

It rained all night with a break in the weather the
next morning. I phoned Animal Control; a man answered and said an officer would meet me where I'd
seen the dog. By late morning, gray clouds sat low in
the sky and occasional wind gusts pushed me along
the cracked sidewalk. Rainwater clinging to a skeletal tree dripped on my now frizzy hair. I waited a few
steps away from the strange lot on Pine Glen. A city

van pulled up and parked near me. Feeling safer with some company, I hurried to introduce myself.

The officer nodded and smiled. Holding it too long in his meaty paw, he shook my hand and introduced himself. Officer Waldo Falk reassured me that the neighborhood had no reports of vicious animals, not even coyotes. A little relieved, I followed him around the lot. He swept the ground with his flashlight as he started toward the cone-shaped structure and waved me back.

"Well, ma'am, this here's an old trash burner. I'll bet lots of strays shelter inside. The dog you think you saw must have left when the rain stopped."

"*Think you saw*?" *Didn't he believe me?* I did not want to meet that dog again or go anywhere near the trash burner, but I did not want this Officer Falk, a tall, solid guy in uniform, to doubt me. I stood next to him about a yard from the burner's threshold, where the dog had disappeared.

"I dunno, ma'am, I don't see any tracks or droppings. I'll have a look inside. You stay here." He rubbed his forehead, messing a frontlet of red hair under the visor of his hat.

I stepped up to the threshold and said, "Maybe the rain washed them away? I saw some bones were over there on the sidewalk last evening. Hey, what's that?" A big pile of something lay opposite the doorway.

"Stop! I told you to wait outside," he barked.

"Okay, okay, I just thought . . ." No use arguing. He was a big man. I retreated, and he disappeared into the cone. Rain was starting up again. Shivering from the damp cold, I pulled my jacket hood over my head. Falk pushed me aside as he rushed out of the trash burner. He pointed me toward the sidewalk. "Get over there, now. Now, I said."

"Why? What happened?" I asked. But the man turned his broad back to me, and I heard only snatches of the intense conversation he was having with someone on his phone. Agitated, he was waving his arm toward the trash burner and pacing as he talked.

A cat appeared out of nowhere and ran across my feet toward the trash burner. Totally bewildered, I chased it inside. Near the wall, the "something" was a mangled human body, its clothing in shreds. One arm, dotted with puncture marks, lay across a pool of blood.

Falk yelled from the doorway, "Get out of there."

I shuddered at the sight of the corpse, so close to my home. My hand shot up to my mouth at the taste of bile. Dazed, I hurried out and ran to the curb. Gusty rain was pelting me. As I turned toward home I heard sirens approaching. Several wailing police squad cars and an ambulance pulled up to the curb. Accompanied by Falk, EMTs rushed into the old incinerator just as the cat dashed out and headed toward me. Sitting at my feet, she—I assumed she was a female because of her small size—had matted, gray fur and odd eyes, blue like those of a Siamese. Probably a stray, I thought.

Police officers joined the emergency crew and were circling the lot with yellow and black barricade tape. "Danger" was written all over it. I'm sure they weren't ironic. Falk joined me again at the curb and gingerly tapped my shoulder. "Let's walk over there to the corner," he said. "It's a good thing you called me. I'm sorry you saw the body. Hard to tell who it was, being so, so—what's the word—messed up?" He licked his lips. "I wish you hadn't gone in."

The cat started rubbing my calves. I patted her flank and Falk frowned at her. He asked, "Yours?"

I gulped. "Oh, yes." At that moment, I did not want this man to nab her. He seemed like a euthanasia fan.

"Well, take her home. This is no weather for an old cat, especially this one." He looked at her with unusual interest. "You should keep her inside and put a collar on her with her rabies tag, otherwise . . ." He shrugged, then he handed me a business card. "Call me tomorrow, after 10 a.m., and I'll update you if I can. But, you know, the police . . . they will probably want to ask you some questions. So, listen, about the dog . . . you don't have to say—" His head swiveled toward an approaching officer and he cursed. "Here comes that cop." He turned back to me and muttered, "I'll get a blanket for the cat. When they finish with you, go right home." He went to his van and returned with a towel. The cat hissed at him as he wrapped her and thrust her into my arms then he returned to his van.

I nodded, overwhelmed and mute. Instinctively, I hugged the cat, who now was nestling against my jacket and purring quite loudly.

The police officer greeted me, his phone in hand. He was a few inches taller than I, solid and graying at the temples, but not close to retirement. "Sorry, ma'am, for all this but I need to ask you a few questions." He showed me his ID. "Detective Ferguson. And you are?"

I told him my name and when he asked me where I lived, gripping the cat in one arm I pointed to my street. "In a four-flat down a couple of blocks, Cedargrove, number 1515."

"Phone number?"

I gave Ferguson my contact information, showed him my ID, and when he asked why I was at that location, I said that while on my walk the previous evening, a vicious dog had threatened me right there. I escaped, but called Falk the next morning to report it, and while we were looking around for the dog, Falk discovered the body in the incinerator.

"A dog, you say?" Ferguson eyed Falk, while jotting all that in a little notebook. He said he'd call later in the afternoon or whenever Forensics gave him the green light. Thanking me, he tipped his hat and returned to the crime scene.

Falk came back and insisted on walking me home if I could wait a few more minutes. He reminded me to groom my "fur baby," as he called her. I watched him stride back to the lot. Heart pounding and with my thoughts in a jumble, I relaxed my hold on Miss Kitty, and she jumped out of my arms. Without another "meow," she ran away. I chased her, but she was out of sight by the time I followed her to the back of my apartment building. I was sorry to lose her, but still, I was glad to get away from Officer Falk.

Shaking from the effects of my adrenaline rush and the cold, damp weather, I sat on the top step of my building's delivery entry under a patio awning. I must have been there lost in my thoughts for quite a while because I jumped when Fanny opened the door behind me. Wrapped in a heavy robe and rubbing her wet hair with a towel, she laughed and said, "You look like a drowned rat. Come inside and I'll brew you a cup of hot tea."

Something about her blue eyes startled me. Then I remembered the cat. "Fanny, I found a cat—just now—but she ran away. She was down by that trash burner."

"A gray female?"

I nodded.

"Oh, she lives around here. I'm glad you've made friends with her." Fanny winked and pulled my arm. Her long, manicured nails were painted blue.

"I guess I did. Anyway, warm tea would be perfect after what I've been through." I followed her down the service corridor and into her apartment.

Fanny draped my wet jacket over the back of a blue wing chair near a radiator and settled into her red sofa opposite me. Still in her chenille bathrobe, she curled her legs under her and blinked at me before asking, "Went out for a walk, huh? Not a great day for it."

I looked around before answering. Her apartment felt smaller than mine, probably because of lots of floor pillows, big, overstuffed chairs, and a plush sofa. Her bed, covered by half a dozen pillows, sat in a deep alcove, closed off from the living/dining room by a pair of sliding glass doors. Her kitchen was small and spare with a microwave oven, a small refrigerator, and an electric teapot. A little primitive for my taste. The hallway leading to the second bathroom was cluttered with large cardboard boxes.

"Fanny, this neighborhood is calm and family-oriented. I didn't expect to see a block of run-down houses so close to us and—of all things—a trash burner, a decaying one, at that!" Out of caution, I did not talk about the corpse.

"Yeah, that's an eyesore, alright. It's a blight on the neighborhood, on site before most of those houses were built. Not used anymore, not as an incinerator." She scratched her ear. "Ready for some tea? How about mint?"

I nodded and rose to help. She waved me back to the sofa and commented, "I heard police sirens while you were out there. Did you see anything?"

I caught my breath. "Well, I actually arranged to meet Animal Control by the trash burner. Because of something that happened during my walk yesterday evening."

Fanny cocked her head and stared at me a bit, then filled two mugs from her teapot. Taking the mug she offered me, I sniffed the light, minty cloud hanging over its rim. "Why would you call them?" she said. "They chase cats and dogs as if they were rats." She licked her lips and took a sip. "Ah." Sliding her mug onto a small coffee table, she stretched her arms over her head. "Much better. Now, tell me more."

Settling into my corner of the sofa, I described the frightening dog and my escape. "Maybe it hated the music coming from my phone," I said. "Whatever, it went into that trash burner. I left and hoped the dog wouldn't follow me. Officer Falk was looking for its tracks this morning when he found . . . found . . . something . . . in the trash burner and called the police."

Fanny's eyes darkened. I could have sworn they were all pupils. "Was it the dog?"

"I don't think . . . you mean inside?"

She picked up her mug and sniffed it again. "The police found a body in there a few years ago. Not identified then. No one from the neighborhood was missing." She sneezed after a few gulps of tea. "Excuse me. I was saying . . ."

"Not from here then?"

"Right, totally unknown. Later . . . the police reopened the case and identified the body. A lawyer, a Loop lawyer, quite famous. Before this, people had gossiped that he had run off with his mistress."

"A lawyer? Do you remember the name and when?"

"Umm, no, I . . . Rothman . . . no . . . Hoffman? No, can't remember the name but it was about three, maybe four years ago. Maybe more. I put it out of my mind."

My heart quickened a little. "My husband died around then."

"Was he a lawyer? Was he murdered?"

"Not murdered; he had a wasting disease the doctors couldn't cure. They think he killed himself. It was bad. And no, he was not a lawyer. He had a commercial real estate firm. I struggled after he died. Our son, too." I felt tears spill onto my cheeks and blotted my nose with the back of my hand.

Fanny put down her mug and scooted closer to me. Humming softly, she put an arm around my shoulders and thrust a box of tissues into my hand. "There, there, I am sorry you went through all that. Would it hurt to tell me how it happened?"

Randy had been so vital for most of our marriage. A daily runner, he loved to compete in marathons all over the globe. Wherever business took him, he'd find a race. He especially loved running with his buddies. He was so fit that his disease caught us by surprise. I explained all that to Fanny and added, "I had loved him, I guess, but later we were spending so little time together." Fanny was staring at me.

"When I look back on it, he was either working, running, or on his damned—excuse me—computer. And I was not athletic—a bit fat, actually. At the end of the day Randy would collapse, exhausted by all his efforts, especially after being online. Anyway, as he worsened"—I shivered, remembering him gaunt and hollow-eyed—"he couldn't bear it, I guess. On our last day together, I had left him bundled in blankets by the TV and met a friend for lunch. Turns out he'd called a cab, was dropped off near the lake, and drowned. That's how they say it went. The police traced the ride, found a note, his shirt and trousers, and some personal items, but no one ever found his body. He disappeared." I didn't mention Lonnie, how close he was to his father. Why complicate the story?

"That's some sad story, but . . ." Fanny wiped her mouth with the back of her hand, grimaced, then made excuses about an appointment. "Sorry, I can't go out dressed like this. Your tea still warm? Take the mug home. I know where to find it," she said while showing me to the door.

"Thanks, Fanny. I appreciate your company . . . and the tea. That business by the trash burner was so strange, wasn't it?"

Fanny whispered, "Strange. Yes. Anyway, you're welcome." She paused and gazed into my eyes. "Be careful around Officer Falk." And she closed the door. I heard her turn the deadbolt.

~

I spent the rest of the day cleaning, always a therapeutic exercise. After mopping the floors, I scrubbed the kitchen counters, stripped the bed, washed and changed my sheets, then poured myself a glass of pinot grigio and sank into my armchair. I swung my feet onto the matching hassock and sighed. A few sips of wine would add a layer of self-medication against my anxiety. I anticipated the sweet sensation of a loosening spine with pleasure. Longing to lean back and close my eyes, I glanced at the digital clock on my kitchen counter to calculate my inevitable nap. Almost 2:00 p.m. The day passed so quickly.

I thought about the morning's strange events, about Fanny's warning, and Falk's rushing me away from the incinerator site. Why scold me about "my" neglected cat when he'd just seen a corpse? Musing, I drifted into a hypnogogic state: a pack of dogs was chasing me. I shrieked "Stop!" and they all sat down, covering their heads with their paws. Just as I saw a big, hyena-like beast emerge from the pack and circle toward me, the phone rang and woke me. I was grateful for its insistent, cheery samba.

Detective Ferguson was calling, asking if I was all right. He thought I sounded frazzled when I picked up.

"Oh, no. I'm fine. Why did you call?"

"Remember my saying I'd call you today? I know it's late, but I'm still here. Would you come to the station house to describe the site, tell us what you saw and heard there? If not this evening, then tomorrow around, say, nine a.m., or is that too early?"

"Not at all. I mean, I can make nine a.m. Where do I go?"

Ferguson gave me the details and I entered them into my phone's calendar. He ended the call by telling me a community alert was going out. The local TV stations were running the story on the evening news and the police department was fielding a lot of calls. "I'd like to hear your side of the story. What does your husband think?"

The morning news. Then Fanny would hear about the body, and so would Dave—if they watched the news.

"No husband. I'm a widow."

"Dammit, no, I mean, I'm so sorry. Thoughtless of me. Anyway, tomorrow at nine."

"Right. See you then."

I hung up and that was that. Oh joy. A trip to the police station. Not hungry yet, I picked up an old *The New Yorker* magazine (a stack of unread issues sat shaming me on my bedside table). Immersed in an essay about a little girl's imaginary friend, I didn't hear anything at first, but after a few sips of wine, noises next door—maybe footsteps, maybe an animal pacing—caught my attention. Hardly more than a month had passed since I last noticed any activity there. I picked up my wine glass and went into the kitchen. I crouched and, peering into the cabinet where I'd repaired the wall, I held my breath and listened.

The sound did come from the other side of the wall. I put down my glass, grabbed my keys, and ran downstairs to Dave's. I banged at his door. King started barking. I called Dave's name, but no one answered. He must have been out.

I crossed the hall to Fanny's and knocked. She didn't respond, either. Alone in the building, I didn't know what to do. Studying Fanny's door, I remembered her warning about Falk. *That's silly*, I thought. Now that I had heard something, Falk would help me. A dog might be abandoned and starving there. I climbed the stairs. Back in my place I found Falk's card on my kitchen counter.

Every so often, the padding sound resumed. I tapped in Falk's number. His voice mail came on. Rather than leave a message, I decided to text him. *Possible abused animal in unit next to mine. Can you investigate? Ella Castle*

In a few minutes, my phone whistled. His text message read: *Will be there ASAP. Address? Unit number?*

I texted back the information and waited in the building's vestibule. Perhaps the stress of moving was catching up with me, but I didn't think I was hallucinating. Or was it the wine? I dismissed the thought. Officer Falk's patronizing tone that morning had made me feel small and silly; but I was in my fifties, able-bodied and energetic. And I knew what I saw—that body brutally torn apart. I argued with myself until I saw Falk's van parked down the block. I left the building and walked over to meet him.

Locking his car, he faced me as I stood on the curb and, without greeting me, said, "You must really be worried about this animal. Where is it?"

"And hello again, Officer Falk. Yes, whatever it is, the problem's been going on for days. I am concerned."

"Okay, show me what's . . . concerning you." He came around the car, grabbed my elbow, and steered me to number 1515. I pulled my arm away and said, "No need to be protective, officer. I'm just fine, but if an animal is in trouble, you're the one to call, right?"

Falk's face did not match his big body. His pointed chin and toothy smile belonged on a fox—a fox with the neck of an ox. "Little lady, you've called the right person. Now let's see what's going on."

As we passed through the vestibule, I spotted Fanny's door, open just a crack. She was watching us but closed the door without a sound when I caught her eye. *That was odd; she didn't answer when I knocked before.*

Falk and I went up to the second floor. Just as we reached the top stair, Dave came out of his apartment.

"Ella," he called up. "What's going on?"

Dave, where were you when I knocked? "Hi, Dave. I thought you were out. I called Animal Control because noises next door started up again."

Falk asked, "Who's he?"

"My downstairs neighbor. Hey, come on up if you like."

Dave looked up, spotted Falk, and waved his hand. "No, thanks, I have to walk King."

With his meaty hand on the banister, Falk leaned over to say, "Hey, wait a minute." But Dave and King were out the door and jogging away. Falk stroked his chin, then turned to face me. "You've probably been hearing his dog all this time. Maybe I should question him."

"No, no. King is a happy pup, but when he sniffed this door"—I pointed to 2A—"he acted terrified of whatever was in there."

"Terrified?" Falk cocked an eyebrow.

"Well, what do you call it when a dog sniffs something, runs back and forth, and raises his hackles?"

"Hmm, usually when he senses competition for a female's attention." Big toothy smile.

This was going nowhere. "Look, officer. I called because I heard noises here that made me worry an animal was trapped inside. I've never seen people go in or out. The downstairs neighbors haven't noticed anyone, either. I think someone has abandoned an animal in there and you need to rescue it."

Falk turned toward the door, knocked, then jiggled the handle. "Looks like no one's home, and . . ." He pressed his ear against the door. "And I don't hear anything in there. Usually, if an animal is in pain—"

The downstairs inner door creaked open. A tall man wearing a hoodie hiding his face was fumbling with keys in the lobby.

I called to him, "Hello? Are you Joe, the maintenance man?"

He nodded but kept his head down. As he walked toward the basement door, I said, "We have a problem in 2A. Mr. Straybill suggested I ask you to open it for me. Would you do that?"

"Not without permission, I can't," he answered so softly I barely heard him.

"Well, I give you permission," Falk boomed. "According to Mrs. Castle, there's probable cause. You have the keys?"

Joe froze and looked up. I glimpsed the end of his nose. He had a short, dark beard. After a long pause, he nodded like a sloth and plodded up the stairs. Keeping his head turned away from me, he pulled a ring of keys from his back pocket. He moved with feral grace toward the door of 2A and unlocked it without a sound. The door swung open.

I stepped closer to peer inside, but Officer Falk threw out his log of an arm to block me and hit me squarely across my chest. I yelled out, "Shit!" I thought I heard a groan inside Joe's hood.

"Geesh, Mrs. Castle, sorry, but you can't go in there. Just me." With a slight nod toward Joe, Falk asked, "You're the maintenance guy for this building?" Falk had whipped out an official-looking notepad and was scribbling something in it as he spoke. "Name?"

Joe whispered something I couldn't catch and turned away. Falk grabbed his shoulder and spun him around. The hood fell back a bit; his scraggly beard covered sharp cheekbones and accentuated large, brown eyes. After glancing at me, Joe pulled up his hood and lowered his head.

"So, Joe, my man, have you noticed anything strange in this building? Mrs. Castle—" Joe began coughing as if a drink had gone down the wrong tube. He wiped his mouth with his sleeve and stepped back. "You okay?" Joe shrugged and cleared his throat. "Fine. Mrs. Castle here says she's heard strange noises in there, like . . . like what, Mrs. Castle?"

I rushed to say, "Scratching, footsteps, or maybe an animal pacing. And a dog whimpering. Not lately, but the pacing resumed today."

"Okay, then. You all wait here. I'll check it out." Falk went into the apartment and closed the door part way. I wished Dave had been there. I decided to have a look anyway. I caught sight of the wall our apartments shared. It had a sink and upper cabinets, but no appliances lined up against it. Just a couple of electric outlets interrupted the expanse, but yellowing wallpaper was peeling. A foot-wide plastered area under the sink was opposite the soft spot I'd patched from my side when I moved in.

Falk was inspecting the place, but when he saw me peering in, he closed the door. I felt a heavy hand on my arm. Joe was pulling me back, whispering, "I recently repaired a crack there." His long, thin fingers were too delicate for such a big man. Shuddering, I vowed never to call this creepy guy to fix anything in my place.

Falk came out. He ordered Joe to lock up and marched all three of us outside. As I left the building and headed toward the sidewalk, I noticed Joe was no longer with us.

Coming up the street with King, Dave waved and called to me. "Everything okay?" Spotting me, King pulled at his leash but, before I could answer, Dave yanked him back. As Falk approached them, King leaned against Dave's leg.

Dave looked away. "Uh, King doesn't like Animal Control. I rescued him from the pound."

"Good citizen, Mr. Dave," said Falk, drawing out his name. I could have sworn he was sneering, but he quickly turned to me. "Mrs. Castle, I'm sure you will be okay. That apartment looks like it's been empty for a long time. It needs a cleaning for sure, but no sign of animal intrusion. Why don't you all contact a pest control company, say for squirrels or mice. Sometimes they move in when a place has been vacant."

Squirrels. "I can't imagine squirrels whimpering. I suppose we first could ask Joe to look for rodents. He was inside earlier."

Dave and King scooted by Falk and went into the building. Moments later, Dave opened the front door and called, "I don't see Joe. He must have left."

Falk poked my shoulder. "You're spooked by my find at the trash burner. Don't worry. We're looking out for that dog you spotted. A stray. It's probably across town by now. Everything's under control. Just keep quiet about the trash burner thing, understand?"

"But the news already—"

He cut me off. "I haven't seen or heard any news story about . . . that."

"But Officer Ferguson . . ."

Falk waved his hand as if he were batting at flies. "Ferguson's a nosy nincompoop."

I'd had enough of Falk's blather. "I don't know about that, but thanks for coming out, officer. I'm sure you have a lot to do besides this."

Falk leered. "Any time for a lovely lady like you."

I didn't smile. Instead, I thanked him again for his help and went back into the building. Dave was waiting for me under the stairwell.

"Hey, Dave. Sorry for all the excitement. What's going on? Did you find something? Where were you when I knocked, if you don't mind my asking."

Dave let King into his apartment, then closed the door. I heard the knob lock click into place. "I was . . . was in the bathroom, I guess." He rubbed his temples. "Anyway, don't apologize. I'm sure you're right. King sensed it, too."

"Well, Falk looked all around, he said, and didn't find anything. I can't imagine what—"

He wrapped his hand around the doorknob. "Oh, crap, I locked myself out."

"Your key?"

"Inside."

"If you can find Joe . . . I mean, he just opened 2A with a master key."

"I'm alright. I think I gave Ms. Katzer a spare." He paused before going out again. "Be careful, Ella."

"Of course," I said with a little flutter in my chest, maybe from excitement, or maybe from fear.

I went up to my landing and, on a whim, turned the 2A door knob. It wasn't locked. At the banister, I watched the glass inner door of the vestibule for a few minutes. Only shadows passed outside. No voices, no footsteps. I put my palm on the door of 2A and pushed, just a little. It swung open.

Twilight filled what might once have been the living/dining room. I felt along the cold and slightly damp wall adjacent to my apartment. When I reached the fresh patch, I crouched for a better view. Just as I switched on my keyring flashlight, I heard a noise behind me. Before I could turn my head, someone hit me hard between the shoulder blades. I yelped and fell forward. My head hit the floor, and twilight turned to midnight.

≈

I groaned at the sound of my name.

"Ella, Ella. What happened? Can you hear me?" A dog was whining and licking my face. The dog next door? I sat up much too fast, and the room spun around. Relieved to see the dog was King, I grimaced and peered at Dave kneeling beside me. My forehead was throbbing. Dave helped me sit up and said, "I heard a scream and a thud just as I came home. What were you doing here? What happened? Look at me. Your head? Let me see. Your eyes are normal. I'd bet-

71

ter call—" He was about to punch a number into his smartphone.

"Don't call 911, Dave. Please. I'm fine. Joe left the door open and—"

"And you decided to look around?"

"I heard a noise. Then something pushed me. The fall knocked me out, I guess."

Dave said he did search for Joe with no results. When he came upstairs to check on me, he saw the door to 2A was open, but no one was around. He looked in and saw me on the floor.

Wobbly, I held onto his arm as I tried to stand. "Would you please stay with me a while? I'm a bit shaken."

He steadied me with an arm around my shoulders and opened my door with the key I took from my pocket. I flipped the light switch.

I couldn't breathe. Someone had ransacked one of the kitchen drawers and had dumped everything on the floor. I limped into my bedroom; they hadn't touched it. Same for my closets and the bathrooms. What did they want? What had they taken? I couldn't imagine.

"This is awful. Who . . . who could have done this?"

"Probably the same jackass who attacked you in 2A. Let me call the police now."

"No, no. I'm seeing Detective Ferguson tomorrow morning. I'll report this to him. It might all be connected."

"I don't know. I think you should report this now." He paused and looked around. "But it's your call." He helped me pick up my corkscrew, stoppers, rubber bands, and other drawer junk and sort things on the counter. I offered him a glass of pinot grigio, which he happily accepted, and he settled into a chair. I poured one for myself and examined the mess.

"The wine should calm you, Ella, but that bump will be a bruise soon. You should ice it."

"I'll deal with that later. I have to see what's missing." As I wiped the drawer and replaced items, I saw that one important object was gone: a small framed photo of Randy from the year before he became ill. I'd kept it in that drawer for those melancholy moments that swept over me once in a while.

Dave cleared his throat. I looked up.

"You look like a kid lost on State Street. Something wrong?"

"My photo's gone . . . a photo I kept of my husband. The only one I have. He didn't like being photographed."

"A photo? Nothing else?"

"No. Nothing else is missing, at least nothing important. But why would someone risk breaking in and take only that?"

Dave shrugged and put his empty wine glass in the sink. Standing next to me, he gave my shoulder a quick squeeze. I shrank back. "Hey, sorry. I just . . . well, just wanted to be there for you. So, two things—

Ms. Katzer had my spare key, and I can go home. You're seeing Detective Ferguson tomorrow?"

I nodded.

"Give him all the details and be straight forward. He's a good guy. We . . . we used to know each other. Why'd you call Falk? I didn't like the way he talked to you."

"Well, I thought Animal Control was the right—"

"Not this time." Dave walked over to the windows, watched the street for a minute, then checked the windows. "This one is open. Please lock them, Ella, and if you want, King and I can walk you to the police station tomorrow."

I was happy to hear that. I told him when I expected to leave, and he asked me to knock on my way out. He said good night and, making a lock-the-door gesture with his thumb and forefinger, smiled and closed the door.

This night was going to be long.

~

At 6:30, the alarm on my radio was playing Prokofiev's *Petrouchka*, the sad parts. I turned over and debated staying in bed; but, no, I had an appointment with Detective Ferguson, and I had to get up. I lowered the volume and went to the toilet. The bathroom mirror offered little comfort. A purple bruise ran along my hairline, more noticeable for the gray bangs framing it. Little shadowy satchels hung under my eyes. Dreams of brutal hunt scenes had punctuated my restless sleep and I shivered as the memory slipped away, although I did remember running with wild dogs after something or someone. Sometimes I was the prey. Each time my rapid heartbeat woke me, I had to catch my breath, look around the apartment, and check the windows. All was quiet. I slipped again and again back under my quilt and hoped for rest. Nothing doing. Another dream, another terrifying wake-up.

After shrugging at my mirror image, I brewed a quick cup of espresso and gazed out the window again. As I sipped my morning remedy, to my left, rounding the corner of my street and Pine Glen Street, where the school stood, I saw a small pack of runners. They were jogging and, in unison, they swung their arms to chin height. A tall, muscular man was leading them. His shouts of encouragement, sounding more like snarls, spurred the group to speed up and they disappeared before I could see more details. Six thirty was my usual wake-up time and, while sipping my coffee, I liked checking out the street below, but that was the first time I'd seen that running group.

I had to tend my bruised forehead, but a warm shower came first. Once dressed I found an old tube of arnica gel. It had helped relieve my bruises in the past, so I smoothed a dab across my forehead. Arnica—the last time I'd used it was after I'd bumped into the mover boxes and tended a big black and blue mark on my knee. And before that, for bruises on my arms.

A week or so before Randy fell ill, we'd had a heated discussion—actually a fierce argument. Something in our exchange inflamed Randy. I thought his eyes had turned red—I do have quite an imagination—and, nearly growling, he had leaped at me from his chair. He raised his fists, and I wrapped my arms around my head to protect it from the blow I expected. He pummeled my arms.

I shouted at him, "Randy, stop. Stop. This isn't you!" He froze. Dropping his arms to his sides, he sank to the floor and wept. The memory of Randy's rage turned my stomach. Before that terrifying moment, although our relationship had cooled, we had shared some interests, like movies and reading, but we had lost the spark keeping us close for so long. Maybe it was his work, his travel, or his preference for jogging and running races. After his illness weakened him and he no longer ran, we hardly spoke to each other. He'd gaze out the window all day and sleep wrapped in blankets on the sofa every night, his chin resting on his folded arms.

I needed to dismiss those thoughts and get ready for my interview with Detective Ferguson. Dressed in black slacks, a white blouse, and my favorite heather-blue cable-knit cardigan, I set off for the district police station. After a glance at 2A, I hurried down the stairs. As I passed her door, Fanny emerged.

"Well, hi. You're up and out pretty early."

"Hi. Yes, an appointment at nine. Have to get going."

Fanny came closer and stared at my face. "Do you mind taking off the hat and sunglasses a sec? Ah, you're hurt. That's a nasty bruise."

Not wanting to upset her, I gave her sketchy information—that I'd fallen, and someone had burgled my apartment while I was knocked out. Fanny replied that she hadn't heard anything.

"That's odd. Dave said he heard me yell and he came to help me."

"You yelled? Why didn't I hear you then? Who did it?"

Her questions annoyed me. Impatient to leave, I said, "Fanny, thanks for caring, but I really have to go. The burglar didn't take anything valuable . . . I mean, nothing worth money. We'll talk later. 'Bye." I patted her arm and left without looking back.

The district police station did not match my expectations. Instead of a squat brick building flanked by concrete pillars topped film noir style with fly-specked globe lights, I entered a recently built modern structure with bright murals on the façade and an open, glass-paneled entrance. Approaching a police-woman at the well-lit reception desk, I told her I had an appointment with Officer Ferguson. She smiled and asked my name. After checking her computer, she invited me to sit on a nearby bench and she would let *Detective* Evan Ferguson know I was on time.

Before I could sit, Detective Ferguson was crossing the lobby. He shook my hand and invited me to follow him into a large room down the hall. Complainants, plaintiffs, or arrestees—hard to tell—sat at five other desks in the room. Detectives interviewing them were entering data into their computers or leaning on one hand while listening to the person opposite them.

Ferguson pulled out a metal chair with wooden armrests and I sat. Since I was wearing slacks, I crossed my legs and leaned back, feigning ease and self-confidence. The detective's tired smile creased his face, especially around his sparkling green eyes.

"Thank you for coming in. I'd like to hear why you were at the trash burner on the date in question and what happened to you there. Please take your time."

I was about to describe my walks around the neighborhood when another detective interrupted me. A tall, scrawny man whose face was etched in a highway map of wrinkles was standing behind Ferguson. He asked if I would like some coffee. I stared at him, then stammered, "Oh, no, thank you. I'm fine."

"You're the Mrs. Castle who called Falk at Animal Control?"

"Pinscher, she and I were—"

"Yeah, yeah, well, ex-*cuse* me. Just being Officer Friendly. Klaus Pinscher, at your service." He gave me a crooked grin and went back to his desk. Settled in his creaking chair, he watched Ferguson and me while ignoring his visitor tapping annoyed fingers on her armrest.

I turned to Ferguson and gave him a confused look. How did Pinscher know my name? Ferguson studied Pinscher for a few moments, then asked me to follow him outside the station house. "You don't have to make a formal statement right now. Let's walk and you can give me some background on all this, okay?"

We strolled through the parking lot until the detective said, "This is far enough. No one can hear us now." I looked around. Clearly, no one was nearby.

"It's fine here, ma'am. We'll have more privacy. You were saying?"

I began again. "I moved here a short while ago, into what I thought was an ideal neighborhood, but . . ." I didn't know how to go on.

"But?"

"Well, one late afternoon, I took a walk." I looked around again, feeling a little spooked.

Continuing to walk, we reached the far end of the station house parking lot, where we shared one of the park benches lining the lot's boundary. He asked me to describe my walk on Pine Glen Street up to the trash burner.

"I love wandering through neighborhoods, especially late afternoon when the low sun makes everything glow." Ferguson's soft smile encouraged me to go on. "I thought it'd be a perfect time to explore the quiet streets near my new home. When I walked past the school on Pine Glen, I noticed how different the houses were there—most were run-down and some abandoned. Just as I neared the lot—"

"Which lot?"

"Why, the one with the trash burner. You know. That's where a dog approached me. Not a nice dog. It had a massive head and shoulders, and it wasn't friendly."

"How so?"

"It growled at me, you know, like a 'I'm-going-to-bite-you' growl, and I worried it would pounce, but . . ." I smiled as I described how the dog lost interest in me at the sound of music playing on my smartphone. I told him about my call to Falk the next morning, about his finding the body in the trash burner and calling the police. "Then you arrived, and you know the rest."

"We came, but not because Falk called us."

"What? But he used his phone to—"

"Actually, someone in the neighborhood, a woman, called about noise—she said she had heard . . ." He paused and pulled his moustache. "She 'heard screaming during the night'—her words—in that lot and asked us to investigate. I thought it was you, but it turns out it was a Fanny Katzer. She lives in your building. Do you know her?"

"Yes. When did she call?"

"A bit before your meeting with Falk that morning. I asked her why she didn't call earlier. She apologized, said she thought it was some teens fooling around. After thinking about it all night she decided it was worse than that and called."

Strange. Fanny heard screaming. I had not. I explained how I knew Fanny. "She and I met a short while ago by our mailboxes. We chatted a bit, and I did tell her about being scared by the dog, then about calling Falk. Turns out she knows him and doesn't like him much, but she didn't mention the noise when we spoke."

Ferguson's mouth twitched and he cleared his throat. "Falk, yeah, well, this isn't his case, although Forensics' report is gruesome, and he could be called in. The victim is—was—a police officer from our district." He paused for a minute while looking around the lot. "Funny that Falk was . . . I mean, the officer was in his running group."

"*His* running group? I saw a bunch of runners pass my place on Cedargrove this morning. Could it be the same one? Detective, what's going on around here? I never expected . . . Can't you give me a clue?"

Ferguson studied the ground for a few minutes. "Mrs. Castle, I can't . . . I'm not supposed to . . . oh, what the hey. This is technically a homicide case, but it looks like canines—coyotes, feral dogs, I don't know what—mauled him. I trust you'll keep this to yourself?"

Shivering I rubbed my arms and started to rise from the bench. "Of course. Not a word. It's just . . .

I thought my neighborhood was peaceful, safe—for being in the city."

"That trash burner attracts trouble, but usually violent crime doesn't happen here. Anyway, please be careful. Here, take this. Call me if you need me." He handed me a business card. I stuffed it in my pocket.

We returned to the station house. He took a short statement, including my suspicions about the noises next door to my place, and offered to have an officer drive me home. I refused politely then called a shared ride and left, my thoughts in a jumble. I had the driver leave me in front of a pizzeria I spotted near Marino's. After picking up a diet soda and a fat wedge of pizza, I found a small table by the window and sat for a while. Each warm bite of the slice—sweet with tomatoes, garlic, and gooey cheese—helped soothe my edginess.

Too many mysteries were interrupting my pizza reverie. Had Fanny followed me on that walk? She knew about the cat, the one appearing out of the blue in the rain, right after Falk found the body. I remembered she was drying her wet hair while talking to me on our back stoop. Was that after a shower or had she been out there, too, in the rain? And she never explained her dislike for Falk—not that she liked Dave either. We were living in a big city, but this neighborhood felt more like a small town, although less and less the ideal Bedford Falls I'd long coveted after seeing *It's a Wonderful Life*. Ferguson's manner soothed my anxieties, but I cringed at the memory of that creepy detective Pinscher who offered me coffee at the station.

~

Home at last, I searched the kitchen for something to cut my thirst; the pizza snack was salty. I changed into a sweatshirt and cargo pants and went to my window with a tall, sweating glass of water in hand. The sound of evenly beating footsteps caught my ear. There they were again, the same pack of runners I'd seen earlier, all heavily dressed in sweatpants and hoodies. They rounded the corner onto my street, apparently from Pine Glen. Was this leg the end of their circuit? That would have been an hours-long run. I assumed they were training for a marathon and nearly turned away from the window when a strange sight pulled me back.

Their lead runner was barking commands, just as he had earlier in the day. His build and manner looked familiar. The leader was Falk. I recognized his red hair and deep-set eyes. Dressed in a T-shirt, shorts, and runner's tights, he more resembled a Marvel Comics superhero than an Animal Control officer. The last runner was lagging behind. The pack stopped so fast in front of my building that they bumped into each other. Falk doubled back, on the far side of the pack. I saw him reach the straggler and slap him hard on the back. I almost dropped my water glass.

Falk sprinted back to the front while bellowing some gibberish. All the runners pressed forward, elbows raised to chest height and sped off. The slow runner broke away. He ran behind a house across the street, through its backyard, and down the alley.

My thoughts went every which way. Wasn't Falk supposed to be working? What was he doing at that hour with those runners? Did he have the day off? Who were all those men?

A call to Ferguson—I had to reach him. He would help me figure this out. I phoned the precinct station and asked for him. The policewoman I had met before my appointment that morning answered my call. I told her I had some vital information to add to my report. She said Detective Ferguson had left the station soon after our meeting and had not returned yet.

"Well, I suppose I could speak with another officer. Which detective would have access to the file Detective Ferguson opened?"

"Detective Pinscher, but he's not here, either. Does Detective Ferguson have your phone number? I could page either or both. I'll take your number in case they don't have it. Then, one of them will get back to you."

"No, please, just Detective Ferguson." After giving her my contact information and thanking her, I ended the call. Restless, I walked to the window again and put my phone on the sill. The little gray cat, my "Miss Kitty," was crossing the street, her tail rigid and parallel to the pavement. She pranced like a cat on a mission. Trotting past an apartment building, she entered a gangway leading to the alley where I'd seen the slow runner disappear. I thought, why not follow her and see where she went, if possible. She might lead me to some clue or other.

My ringing phone rattled against the wooden sill. Hoping it was Ferguson, I glanced at the caller ID. It said "Chicago." I was about to decline, thinking it was some kind of scam call, but curiosity won. I answered. It was Dave.

"Hey, Ella, just calling to see how you are. I was going to walk you to the police station this morning, but you didn't knock. I was worried."

"Oh, thanks, Dave. I'm sorry. I was so obsessed with the interview, I just forgot."

"But you did meet with Ferguson? What did you think of him?"

"Respectful. A good listener. Mostly, it went well. Hey, can I ask you a question?"

"Sure. What's up?"

"Have you noticed a running group on our street? About six thirty every morning?"

Dave took his time to answer. "No, that's way too early for me. I have my first coffee around seven thirty." He laughed. "Anyway, what's so strange about a bunch of runners around here?"

I felt uneasy for a moment. I did not know Dave, really. How would he take this next bit? Squelching my doubts, I said, "They ran by here just now. I recognized that Animal Control officer leading the group."

"I didn't hear them go by. I'm a deep sleeper. Did you say Falk, the Animal Control guy?"

"I did. Anyway, my new cat friend just ran away to Pine Glen, I think. I'm going over there to see if I can catch her."

Dave chided me for risking another bad trash burner experience. I said I wasn't worried about it, not since Animal Control and the local police were aware of the dog. He insisted on walking with me if I was so determined to go.

"You don't have to do that. I'm just looking for a cat."

"Oh, but I want to."

I smiled involuntarily. "Okay, Dave." I had to trust someone besides Detective Ferguson. "Thanks. Give me a few minutes, and this time I won't forget to knock."

Dave laughed again. "Good. Can King come along?"

"I don't know about that. You know, like the saying, 'fighting like cats and dogs'?"

"See you soon." He hung up.

I put my phone in my deepest cargo pants pocket and went to the bathroom for a quick pee and a lipstick repair.

❧

When King lunged toward the trash burner, Dave lost his footing and fell. The dog ran ahead, his leash dragging behind him. He paced across the open doorway and, eyeing us, barked in short, loud yaps. Dave sat up, wincing at the cuts on his palms and at the ripped knees of his jeans. He looked up at me, and I noticed new shadows under his eyes.

"Ella, please get King away from there."

I reached for his arm. "Are you hurt, Dave? Can I help you up? Maybe King smelled the cat?"

Dave brushed away my hand. "I'm fine. I'm fine. Just a few cuts. Nothing serious. Would you grab King's leash?"

Would King have been so upset about a cat? Obviously something else inside the incinerator was bothering him. Dave was struggling to stand. I said, "Okay, I'll get him." I called to King, "Here, boy, come." The dog would not move. I raised my voice. "Come, King." Instead of trotting back to me, King stood just outside the trash burner. Growling, he lowered his head and pawed the dirt under his feet.

I sighed and scanned the area as I approached the dog. For a moment, I thought a curtain moved in the rear window of the frame cottage next to the lot, the same dimly lit window I'd noticed when I first explored Pine Glen. I heard Dave groan as he was levering himself up by one knee. I shrugged and kept going. When I reached King, I squatted to pick up his leash lying among discarded wrappers and crushed beer cans. The dog was pawing at two grooves in the dirt that led into the incinerator. I glanced back at Dave who was limping toward me. Curious about the grooves, I went inside. The plastic leash handle cut into my palm as I screamed.

His head was unscathed but the rest of Detective Ferguson's body was twisted as if some giant hands had wrung him like a wet washcloth. Nauseated, I couldn't speak, but my scream must have done the job. Dave ran to my side, his own wounds forgotten.

"What the friggin' hell are you—" The dog was sniffing Ferguson's remains. "Stupid dog, get back." Dave gagged and retched into the bag he'd intended for King's poop. Stunned at first by Ferguson's mangled body, I had not moved. I was staring at the detective's rolled-back eyes and gaping mouth. I kneeled and lowered my cheek over his mouth and nose. No breath. His wrenched torso was still. I held his wrist. No pulse. "He's gone, Dave. Dead. Oh, I'm so sorry. He was a friend of yours, wasn't he?"

Dave wiped his mouth with his sleeve. "He is—he was. I should call this in, but I can't let the police find me here. Hey, what's that?" An approaching police car siren silenced us.

Dave stowed his phone in a hip pocket and whispered, "Outside, Ella. Hurry." We brushed debris from our clothes and hid behind the trash burner. "The siren. Who could have . . . it's not possible. Why'd *they* be coming here, I mean, now?" His eyes were so big. After looking around he pointed to the frame cottage. "Move, quick. To those back steps."

We ran to the far side of the cottage, and I crouched behind the steps' concrete base. I said, "Maybe they aren't coming here. Someone could've reported a mugging or something." As Dave said, how could anyone have alerted the police about the murder before we discovered Ferguson?

"Mugging? Unlikely. Other than those bodies in the incinerator, nothing ever happens around here."

"Except the noises next door to me, and whatever attacked me in 2A." I wanted to say, "Dave, believe me now; something bad has been happening around here." But I didn't. Instead, I grabbed his sleeve as he moved away from the steps toward the alley.

"Listen," he rasped. "I'm going to run for it. What about you?" He shook off my hand. He looked a lot more afraid than I felt. Not knowing how to answer, I shrugged. Dave patted my shoulder and, poop bag in hand, ran down the alley with King, who kept pulling away from him and looking back at me. Oh, yes, my big protector.

Hiding in a dark corner, out of sight and feeling brave, I waited a while to see where the police were going. If they came to the trash burner lot, I planned to hide, then dash home as soon as they'd left.

The first police cruiser pulled up. I crouched behind the stairs. My chest felt tight, and I was breathing too quickly. I wished Dave were still with me. Was he heading home or someplace else? I stopped my anxious musings at the sound of a soft whistle over my head.

"Pssst."

I looked around.

"Hey, up here." At the top of the weathered stairs, Joe was standing in a darkened doorway. "Better come in . . . Mrs. Um . . . Mrs. Castle. Before Pinscher spots you."

I could just make out Detective Pinscher easing out of the car. I did not want to deal with him again. Turning to face Joe, I saw him go in and I followed.

So, that's how Red Riding Hood's grandmother felt in the wolf's belly—trapped. Joe was standing in shadow next to a kitchen sink. He waved his hand toward a metal folding chair. "Stay still," he whispered as he watched the street. I blamed myself for not running home with Dave, but I wanted to know why the police arrived without our calling. Did Joe phone in the murder? My head throbbed. I rubbed my neck and felt my pulse racing.

I crumpled into the chair Joe pushed toward me. The whole house was dark except for weak afternoon light framing the edges of thick curtains. Joe's hood covered most of his face, but I stared at his long, tapered fingers in silhouette against the light. He had what I liked to call musician's hands, able to reach with ease beyond a piano keyboard octave. His hoodie shaded his face, but his other hand, tightly knotted in a fist, betrayed his mood, which was, what? Anger, anxiety—or murder.

Afraid to speak, I waved to get his attention and pulled my phone out of my purse. Opening the Notes app, I typed, *What's going on?* He read it and, pushing his palm down, he shook his head as if to say, *Don't ask me now.* I relaxed a little. If Joe wanted to hurt me, he would have done so by now. I stiffened again. *Or maybe not. Maybe while the police were near, they would hear my screams, so he was waiting until they left.* I stood up and turned toward the door. Joe grabbed my sleeve and said in a low growl, "Sit! Please. And be quiet. I won't hurt you." He looked out the window again after I sat.

We must have stayed like that for more than an hour—me clutching the seat of my chair, Joe peeking from behind the curtain. "Someone's pulling a gurney," he said. A shout came from the trash burner lot, and I jumped—Pinscher's oily voice cut through the gurney's squeaking through the gravel. "Watch it, Price. Keep it covered. Carson, check out the house."

Running footsteps crunched toward Joe's cottage, then thumped the front steps. Joe stepped back from the window and crouched next to me. With a finger begging my silence, he dropped to his hands and knees and crawled into the living room facing the street. Bracing his back against the wall, Joe slid to the floor as Carson's fist hit the front door, barricaded by a large desk, barely visible in the gloom.

Carson bounced down the stairs. I heard him circle the house while beaming his flashlight at the windows. "Looks like no one's home, sir," he yelled and ran back to the burner lot.

Joe ducked into the kitchen and peered out the window again. "They're leaving," he said and sank to one knee. I heard him mutter, "What's the rush, guys?" He turned toward me. "They took the body away without collecting evidence, like they wanted to hide something." He sighed and pushed the hood off his head. "Fine, it's time we had a talk." His head and thick curls were silhouetted against the street-lit curtains.

I said, "I should be going, really."

"No, you shouldn't."

Now the accumulation of all those little insults I'd been feeling since I met up with that nasty dog burst out. I screeched, "And why not? Tell me what's been going on out there, not to mention apartment 2A." I stood and backed my way to the kitchen door. "I just wanted to move into a nice, quiet place. Look what I got." I took a deep breath. After all, Joe had taken me in. "Anyway, thanks for keeping me safe from the police, but can't you just leave me alone?"

"I can't. Because you're not Ella Castle. Your last name is Volkman." He stood and stepped closer. With his hand on the door, he whispered, "Please stay. We really have to talk."

How did he know my married name? That hand—familiar. But his shadowed face, so hard and. . . My curiosity outweighed my rage. Rocking between anger and anxiety, I returned to the chair and sat, leaning forward, with my hands on my knees. I would see this through. "Alright, whoever you are, talk."

～

His head bowed, Joe sat cross-legged on the linoleum floor, a small battery light in his lap. He cleared his throat, pushed back the hood, and, after wiping his mouth with a shaking hand, said, "First of all, my name isn't Joe."

"What? I mean, I don't understand."

Wiping his eyes, he muttered something like, "This is so hard." His head sank lower.

"Joe, or whoever you are, please speak up. I can't hear you."

"It's me, Lonnie." He raised his head and shined the light on his face.

Those soft brown eyes, my son's eyes, but the beard? My head was spinning. "Lonnie? How can you be? He lives in London. What are you doing here?" I was breathing fast, and words struggled to pass my lips. "Your hands, yes . . . but your face . . . where have you been?"

He flipped off the lamp switch and we sat in dark silence for a while until he scooted back against the wall and said, "I've been here for years. Right here. For too long." He snorted and dropped his chin.

"In this house? Before I moved into the neighborhood?"

"Yes."

"Did you call the police just before?"

"No, I didn't call the police. I don't know who did or why they came. And, no, I didn't murder anyone. No, never." He seemed to read my mind.

"Then who? I mean, I couldn't imagine you . . . Oh, Lonnie."

My thoughts were jumbled. They skipped from Lonnie's lies and the realization I'd moved by chance into his neighborhood, to the wild idea that maybe Randy's story has a different ending. As if in response to that last thought, I heard footsteps thumping down the stairs. They weren't Randy's; they weren't human. The dog that menaced me on my first walk down this block was standing in the kitchen doorway.

The chair fell back as I jumped up. It clattered to the floor, but the dog paid no attention. He padded over to Lonnie's side and lay next to him on the cracked linoleum floor. Raising his shaggy head, he stared at me with large black eyes. Quivering from a surge of adrenaline, I could barely stand, and I leaned against the wall. Did my short breath mean a heart attack was on its way?

After patting the dog's head and telling him to stay, Lonnie righted the chair. He steered me by my shoulders and sat me down again. "I can explain all this, but it will take some time—time you don't have right now. Straybill will be looking for you, so you'd better go home."

"But—"

"No buts. I'll make like I've come to fix that patch in your kitchen, and we can talk in your place, when Straybill's not around."

With an image in mind of Fanny Katzer peeking round her apartment door, I asked, "What about Fanny? She has her eyes on everything that goes on."

"Oh, Fanny, well, you'll tell her I'm there to fix something." Walking me to the back door, he added, "How about ten a.m.? I'll let myself in?"

Those last words chilled me. "Let yourself . . . I mean, have you been able to . . ." I squeezed my temples. "Lonnie, I don't know what to think."

Hesitating at first, he tapped me on the back, like a falling leaf grazing my spine. "I haven't done what you're thinking." He opened the door slowly and looked out. With a glance at the dog whose head-bob resembled a nod, he showed me out and urged me to go along the alley. I hesitated, grieving for whatever had happened to him over the last few years, then left without looking back.

~

The windows of Dave's condo were dark. Did he say he was running home? Maybe not if he was avoiding the police. Back in the trash burner, he had seemed as surprised and horrified as I felt to find Detective Ferguson's mangled body. A few days before, he had urged me to talk to Ferguson, said he was a good guy, that they were friends.

I dashed upstairs without a glance at the mailbox or my neighbors' units and switched on my hall light as I entered. Thankful to find everything in order, I went to the bathroom, relieved myself at last, and washed my hands and face. Studying myself in the mirror, I winced at the reflection of my reddened eyes. I'd been weeping all the way home. Used a lot of tissues, which I pulled out of my pocket and tossed in the bathroom trash basket. Something else fell in the basket—Ferguson's card. Another surprise, one that shook my hand holding the card. On the back he'd written, "Whatever happens, do NOT call Falk again."

In a daze, I paced my place from living room to bedroom and back again, then ended in the kitchen. Ferguson's card was still in my hand. I put it on the counter and opened the fridge. Low blood sugar. That was it. I hadn't eaten much all day. Bread and cheese would help. I sat on my high stool and ate soothing soft garlic goat cheese on crispbread, one bite after another until my steady hands could close the cheese tub with a snap. Picking up the card, I re-read Ferguson's message. Did he write it before our appointment? He must have known something bad about Falk—not that I thought much of that arrogant blowhard. And now Ferguson was dead. After talking to me. I paced through my apartment again.

No good vibes had passed between Falk and Ferguson the morning I reported the dog by the trash burner—they acted wary of each other. And that dog—I shivered—it was Lonnie's dog after all. Not threatening this time. Why did it threaten me before? I rested at my desk for a while, staring at my laptop until it booted up. I clicked on my browser and searched "dog breeds." Image after image yielded nothing like Lonnie's dog. My eyes burned.

After washing up and putting some drops in my eyes, I fell into bed and did not wake up until just before dawn. I heard someone scratching on my door. Still in my clothes from the previous day, I ran a comb through my hair and tip-toed to the front door. Through the peep hole, I saw Fanny Katzer. She was leaning over the landing's railing. I opened the door.

"Fanny, what's wrong? It's only six o'clock. Sun's not quite up yet."

"It's Straybill."

"What? Dave?"

"I heard King barking and whimpering. Thought I'd better check. He was outside my door and making quite a racket. I don't like dogs but I felt sorry for him."

"Why? What's going on?"

"Straybill's door was open but he wasn't there."

King bounded up the stairs, his leash dragging behind him, and stood shivering next to Fanny. I asked her to come sit in my armchair and have some tea. She demurred and muttered again about Dave abandoning his dog. I found the bag of treats I'd stowed in my utility closet and put some in a saucer for King. He eyed them and turned away. Trotting to the French windows, he pawed the panes and cried.

I cupped my hand under his jaw and whispered, "Sit, King. It's okay. It's okay. I'll look out there."

He sank onto his front paws and waited while I unlatched the windows. Stepping out on the balcony, I scanned the street still dimly lit by decorative streetlamps. Without a sound, Fanny arrived next to me. She leaned over the wrought-iron railing, sniffed, then pointed below.

"Don't you see him?" She hissed, I swear, from the sides of her mouth as she pointed to a dark clump under my neighbor's balcony. "Come on."

Grabbing my keys and flashlight, I followed her downstairs to the front lawn. King rushed to the mass Fanny had spotted and started barking and pawing at it. My flashlight revealed Dave's face.

"Dead?"

Without moving him, I felt for his neck pulse and breath. He was alive but unconscious. Scanning him with my flashlight, I could see that, unlike Ferguson's body, Dave was lying in a fetal position, nothing twisted or awry. I patted his head and pulled back after touching a warm, sticky spot just above his neck.

"His head is bleeding, Fanny."

"I called 911." As she put her phone back in her jacket pocket, I glimpsed her fingertips, tipped with curving blue nails.

"Fanny, do you—"

"We have to help Dave now. You take King to your place. If Dave goes to the hospital I'll follow the paramedics."

"You have a car? How—"

"I can manage." She swiveled and stared up the street. If she had been a dog, I'd swear she was pricking her ears at that moment. "They're coming. I hear their siren."

"I don't hear anything."

Kneeling close to Dave, she bent her head to his chest and purred—or I thought she was purring, but an approaching ambulance masked the sound. By the time the EMTs arrived and silenced their siren, Fanny's "purring" had stopped. I wondered what she had been whispering in his ear. Convinced stress was fooling my senses, I left them and brought the emergency team, a young man and a middle-aged woman, to Dave. He was groaning as his frenzied dog pawed his leg and licked him.

Fanny stood up and hissed at King. "Get back, dog." King shrank away from her. I struggled with King's leash while the pair examined Dave's wound. With a labored grunt, he sat up and tried to push them away. Fanny knelt beside him and murmured something that must have been helpful, because he nodded and let them proceed. After they took his blood pressure and checked his eyes and pulse, they offered to take him to the hospital, but he refused. "No need. My friends'll take care of me. It's nothing. I just fell over . . . over . . ." He spotted a garden hose on the lawn. "Over that. It was dark."

The woman paramedic asked again if they could take him to the hospital. "Now that you are conscious and alert, you may refuse transport, but . . ." She eyed Fanny, then me. "Friends of this gentleman? What happened?"

We explained that we had been searching for him and found him there unconscious. I suggested someone in the ER could better assess his wound, but Dave pressed his lips together and waved the emergency team away.

"It was an accident. I'll be fine. 'Preciate your help." Dave leaned back on an elbow. After palpating his wound, he winced at his bloody fingertips and rubbed his forehead with his clean hand.

Fanny wiped his fingers with a tissue and blurted, "I'm a trained nurse. I can dress his wounds." Well, that was a surprise. I was learning something new— and puzzling—about her every time we were together. Puzzling because when I first met her, she had nothing nice to say about Dave. Now, kindness nearly oozed out of her.

After Dave shakily signed a waiver, the EMT team packed up and left. We helped him stand and walk to the door. King ran ahead of us. Inside the lobby, Fanny handed me Dave's keys. "Take care of King. I'll see to Dave."

"Wait, I can help, I—" They went into Fanny's place and she closed the door without turning back. King scratched at the door, but I soothed him and coaxed him into Dave's place. Remembering where Dave kept the dog chow, I poured out some pellets, and King dived into his bowl. While he chomped with pleasure, I snooped a little. Dave's desk was close to the kitchen area. Next to his printer, I saw several scattered sheets. Curious, I scanned one with headings in bold dividing the dense text into several categories, one of which was Runners' Club.

The papers comprised notes, some in typeface and others handwritten, but this one was about the runners I'd seen in our neighborhood, runners Dave protested he'd never noticed. Most of the notes were observations: how many runners, their identities (with "Falk" underscored in rough dashes), the direction of their movement, the leader (Falk again), and times of day. So, Dave wasn't one of them, but he knew them and was watching them. For whom?

Someone was knocking on his door. I tried to arrange the papers as I had found them, then I tiptoed to the door and peeked through the peephole. Dave's arm was draped over Fanny's shoulder as she guided him in and lowered him to the couch.

"Swing up your legs. That's it. Now lean back while Ella makes you some coffee." Fanny eyed me, then the kitchen. She fussed with the cushions until she deemed his feet sufficiently elevated.

I filled the water reservoir and, finding Dave's stash of capsules, brewed him a quick cup. "Here you go, Dave. A nice cup of Italian fortissimo." As I handed him the coffee, he looked up at me. "Thanks. Sorry I deserted you back there on Pine Glen. The local police make me nervous."

Fanny narrowed her eyes. "You left Ella alone with the police? When? Why?"

He nodded, slugged back the coffee, and held out his cup for a refill. "Please. That's just what I needed. Yes, Fanny, we had a scare last night and I panicked."

Dave had no trouble talking now. Although I sent Fanny a quizzical look, she avoided meeting my eyes. Abruptly, she wished Dave a speedy recovery, and left me to take over.

With King circling nearby, Dave smiled broadly. "Thanks, Fanny. You've been kind. I'm fine now. Okay with you, Ella? Anyway, I should explain a few things to you."

As I nodded, Fanny was already out the door. I locked it, made another espresso, and wheeled Dave's desk chair next to the couch. "Like you haven't been straight with me?" I waggled my finger as I sat. "Turn around. Let me see your head." I scooted the chair closer to the couch.

Dave shifted his torso and bared his neck; his wound was clean and closed.

"You have a great immune system, or whatever."

He started to feel the wound but stopped short of tapping the base of his skull. "Fanny said not to touch. She's something else, I guess. A really good nurse."

"I didn't know she was trained."

"Me, neither." He sipped his coffee this time and gazed at me for a minute before inviting me to make a cup for myself. "Sorry. I wasn't thinking."

"No, that's fine. Don't need the caffeine." I inhaled a deep breath. "So, what did you want to tell me?"

He sat up straighter, lowered his feet to the floor, and cleared his throat. "I wasn't straight-forward with you. I have seen the runners' group go by early in the morning. You recognized Falk, right?"

I nodded.

"He leads them around the neighborhood. If I'm out that early with King, I sometimes catch them coming or going from Pine Glen. Not the most scenic route."

"Right. So, you have been watching them."

He nodded. "As I said."

This conversation was going nowhere. I leaned toward him. "I don't understand why you lied to me."

Dave stood up, wobbled a bit, then went to his sink and washed out his cup. He emptied the capsules into a recycle bin and stood quite still. I waited.

"Not exactly lied."

"Yes, exactly. As if I were crazy to even worry about them."

"Well, not crazy. I just didn't want you to be involved."

"Involved? In what?"

He rubbed the top of his head, then sat down on the couch. The cushions creaked. Facing me, he said, "It's out of my hands now. You are actually involved, with the two homicides, the dog, all that—and Falk. And what's with the name Ella Castle? Your rental agreement says Ella Volkman."

I jumped up and walked over to the desk. My hand on his notes, I yelled, "You've been spying on a lot more than those runners."

Dave pushed himself slowly off the couch. Tapping the papers on his desk, he said. "Oh, I see how you—"

"Uh-huh, you're taking notes on them." I stood as straight and impressive as I could make myself. "Who are you, Dave? More than just a nice guy who lives downstairs." Propping himself on the edge of his desk, he leaned back and said, "I've lived here for quite a while. Moved here with my wife from Evanston, near the university. I was studying there." Dave had grown up on the south side of the city, gone to a private high school, then Amherst College.

I said, "Who knows, we might have known each other as kids, because until high school, I lived in the same area."

"Oh yeah? Public school?" When I nodded, he asked which one and it turned out we'd been at Kenvale Elementary at the same time. "Wild, but I don't remember a girl named Ella," he said and explained about Evanston. He'd studied at the Center for Public Safety, then stayed in the suburb for a few years.

"That's an advanced police training facility, right?"

"More than that—"

"So, you're a cop?"

"An undercover homicide police detective. I'm assigned to a case where someone died and foul play's suspected." He let that sink in.

I stood up. "Think I'll have that espresso now."

He followed me into the kitchen. He poured fresh water into the reservoir. I chose a "forte" from his basket of capsules, and he pressed the lever. As I warmed my fingers around the cup and sipped the steaming brew, he said, "I actually was assigned to the alleged homicides in the trash burner. I think someone knows my connection to the case and attacked me when I came home last night."

I nearly dropped my cup. "They tried to kill you?"

"Maybe."

"Is Straybill your real name?"

"No. Like you, I'm undercover." He smiled, then examined his nails.

"Your real name?"

"Can't say."

"Not fair."

"That's life."

I sat again on the couch. When he said, "trash burner," I remembered Lonnie was coming to my place that morning. I was dying, excuse the expression, to find out more from Dave, but my son came first. "Dave, you've dropped a bomb in my lap, but I can't process it now. The building's handyman—you know, Joe. He's coming by this morning to patch the wall behind my sink. I need to go now." I hiccupped. "You know, I want to straighten up my place before he arrives. Can we talk later, maybe before dinnertime?"

Still leaning back on his desk, Dave nodded. "Okay. Sure. Where?" He waved his hand at the dishes. "Please, don't fuss with the cups. Oh, and since you're talking to Joe, have him unlock 2A for me? I'd like to look around again."

I stared hard at him. *Again*? Oh, right, he'd found me there when someone knocked me out. But who? Shrugging I said, "I don't know, Dave. Joe unlocked it because Falk bullied—" I couldn't finish. Lonnie and Falk. What was going on? I left the cup on his counter. "How about we meet at this place around five thirty?" I took a blank sheet from a pad on his desk and scribbled an address a world away from our neighborhood—Caitlin's on the near South Side. It was where my office pals and I used to go about once a week.

"Sounds good. I like the South Loop vibe. Meet you inside?" He tapped my hand holding his pencil.

"Ah, here. I almost walked off with it. You'd nab me for theft." I waited for a smile. He only nodded. "No, really. I'll see you at Caitlin's." His good-bye was a brief wave, as if he were batting a fly.

Back in my place, I spotted a note pushed under my door. I carried it over to the window and unfolded it. *Reminder—See you at 11:00. Don't worry. Love L.*

My finger caressed the letters. The first hand-written words I'd had from him in years. My phone screen said I had less than 30 minutes to tidy up. I put on a pot of decaf, cleaned up the sink and counter, pulled my armchair close to my sleek Ikea couch, and then realized I had not told Fanny about "Joe's" visit. I grabbed my keys and dashed down to Fanny's.

She didn't answer my furious knocking. I turned toward the vestibule at the sound of someone shouting. It was Fanny, arguing with Lonnie.

"I don't care if you do have a key. I don't know you and you can't—oh, hello, Ella. This man says he's our handyman and has come to fix something in your place. Well?"

Twitching his lips, Lonnie gave me a faint smile. I said, "Yes, this is Joe, our handyman. Joe, Fanny Katzer. Not to worry, Fanny. I did ask him to fix something in my place."

Letting out a slow, soft hiss, she scanned Lonnie. "I smell dog on you. I don't like dogs . . . much. Well, it depends. Oh, the heck with it." Fanny unlocked the inner door and held it for us. "Mind you, Ella, any problems, you call me."

"Sure thing, Fanny. I'll scream. Maybe you'll hear me this time."

She sniffed and banged shut her apartment door.

Glancing after her, Lonnie followed me upstairs. I told him to leave his tool kit by the door and sit on the couch. He looked around, stroked the couch's tight gray upholstery, and said, "You've changed your whole esthetic, Mom. All contemporary—" He spotted my armchair. "Except for that. You kept it."

Mug of coffee in hand and settled into my big old chair, Lonnie stroked the soft fabric covering its arms. He spent the next half-hour unraveling his life as a college drop-out. He'd never been an enthusiastic student, although a bit of a jock in high school.

Cross-country running had been his passion. He'd run for hours after school, bolt down the dinner I'd saved for him, and spend the rest of the evening in his room. I assumed he was doing his homework because he enrolled in the state university.

Not at the top of his class, but good enough, Lonnie stayed there for a couple of years. Randy died and Lonnie said in emails that he'd dropped out to work for a friend in London. His emails were vague about the kind of work he did, but it sounded like he was writing copy for a realtor there. When he'd left for England, we had not been on the best terms. Everything I did was wrong. Randy had been his hero.

Until yesterday, I had assumed Lonnie's rare emails were from London. Now, my son was telling me that before Randy died Lonnie had been working for him on a property Randy managed in town. Meanwhile, with my husband gone and a son far away—an aching loneliness had set in. Pointing that out to Lonnie, while we sipped our decafs, I saw his hand tremble as he placed his mug on my IKEA tray table, next to an uneaten brownie. He leaned back, dipped his chin into his chest, and mumbled something.

"What did you say, Lonnie?"

"Dad . . . well, Dad . . . um, he was in trouble then." Lonnie raised his head and forced himself to look squarely at me. "Before his illness. Dad was managing the sale of a large tract for a planned development. You know, with townhomes, high-rises, retail, maybe a hotel. He found out the developer wasn't on the up and up. Dad pulled out of the deal. The developer threatened to curse him. Dad laughed it off."

"Of course. How could he take that seriously?"

"He should have."

"What do you mean?"

"The curse, it was real."

When I'm so stressed I can hardly think, I go through my fridge or kitchen cabinets for relief, but the thought of a curse killing Randy stifled that impulse. I threw my brownie in the garbage and stood in front of Lonnie's chair. Fearing my son was inventing a scenario to cover his own failures, I said, "Are you on something? There's no such thing as a real curse."

I backed away as Lonnie stood and began to pace the room. "Mom, I don't *use* anything. I'm—surviving. Dad did suffer from a curse, but worse things happened before it began to ruin him—sort of."

I sat again on the couch, now sorry I tossed that brownie. I needed thick, chocolaty comfort. "*Sort of?* He died. That's what it looked like."

"Yeah, it was meant to look like that."

I remembered how only a few of his possessions remained scattered on the bluff, how neither divers nor the public found his body, and how much his suicide seemed certain. "What really happened, Lonnie?" My pulse was near fibrillation speed. "Is Randy dead . . . really dead?" Racing thought: was I a widow or not?

Lonnie stopped pacing. He walked to the windows and closed the blinds. Leaning against my counter, he said, "I can't tell you. I mean, he disappeared, but he made sure I had a place to live and a job."

"In that wretched house? As a neighborhood handyman with a strange, scary dog?"

He stared at me for too long before answering, "Yes, with that dog."

"Were you living there when I thought you were in London?"

He cleared his throat and pointed to our plates. "Let's clean up. I can't stay. Neighbors will wonder."

He carried our mugs into the kitchen, cleaned out the coffee pot, and put it on the dish rack, then swept crumbs off the counter into the garbage. "If Straybill sees that you entertained me—that is, if you've been letting him in . . ." Lonnie frowned. "He shouldn't think it was a social occasion, you know."

"Right, but—dammit, Lonnie—when are you going to explain all this?"

"Tonight. Use the alley. Come to my back door. We'll be waiting for you around—"

"*We?* Oh, you and that dog. Anyway, I can't, not tonight. Dave and I are meeting for a drink at Caitlin's. By the way, please unlock 2A so he can look around. He says he's working on the trash burner murders. He could be on our side."

Lonnie rubbed his face, then clenched his fists. "I doubt it. Be careful. Don't tell him about me."

"I wouldn't dream of it."

"Okay, then tomorrow, after dark, around six?" I nodded as he opened the door and said loudly, "I understand, Mrs. Castle, I'll be back in a few days to check on it."

He unlocked 2A and ran down the steps. Following him, I called out "Thanks . . . Joe." Nothing much was in my mail box—a few flyers and an electric bill. I watched Lonnie cross the street, skirt the building opposite mine, and trot down the alley. *My son, who would have thought?*

As I turned to go upstairs, Dave was leaving his place with King tugging at the leash. I waved and started up the stairs. Dave tapped my arm as I gripped the banister. Without a thought, I sighed and pulled back as if from a flame. "Hey! Are you all right? That was quite a sigh," he said.

"Oh, I turned too fast, that's all." A surge of heat rushed from my head to my chest. I had to get away, calm down, be rational about this. "I'm fine, Dave. I'll see you later, and Joe unlocked 2A." Not waiting for a response, I studied each slow step up. After locking my door, I slid to the floor, tears running down my cheeks. A tornado of questions blasted through my brain. Most of all, questioning whom to trust—Dave or Lonnie or neither. What else would Lonnie tell me about Randy? Where was he hiding if still alive?

~

Caitlin's was an old, dark bar with a few high tables along a brick wall. Near a repurposed railway station, it sat in a gentrified neighborhood formerly serving several printing and publishing companies dependent on the materials trains used to transport into the city. The evening I met Dave there, it was cold, with the nip of imminent snow in the air—too soon for October. Intending to pay for my own beer, I stopped at the corner ATM. As I tucked a few twenties into my wallet, I saw Dave coming around the corner, probably from the subway stop nearby. I caught up with him close to the tavern.

"Hey, Dave."

"Ella!" he said with a big grin. No man had been that happy to see me since I dated Randy.

"Well, who else?" I said with a frown, still rattled by Lonnie's revelations.

He cocked his head and pointed his open palm toward Caitlin's. "Shall we?"

I nodded. We went up two steps through a double door into a space built in the late 1800s. It smelled as if spilled beer had lacquered the floor for over 100 years. The high-top table and chairs we found were comfortable enough. Dave went to the bar and brought back a Guinness for me and some bottled craft beer for himself.

"I like it really hoppy," he said, licking foam off his lip. "You like Guinness? I mean, is that what you usually drink?"

"I don't, *usually*. When my work pals and I used to come here, I drank Guinness. It feels like a meal, actually. So dense, filling, you know? Hey, I could be an ad."

Dave adjusted himself in his chair and, after another sip, said, "Yeah. So, Ella, I have some information for you. A surprise, really, for me—actually, about your husband."

I nearly coughed up my Guinness. Too many revelations in one day. Settling my glass into its wet puddle on the scarred wood table, I leaned back and forced myself to look directly at him. Under the table, my fingers were strangling each other. "Who?"

"I know you are using your maiden name, Castle. Your married name was Volkman. And you are acquainted with Officer Waldo Falk, right?"

I nodded with a grimace. "Uh, we'll never be best buds."

"Well, here's another surprise for you. A Randy Volkman used to contact Waldo Falk and Klaus Pinscher."

My finger traced circles around the wet base of my Guinness. After taking a shaky sip, I said, "What, Falk *and* Pinscher?"

"Steady there. I—uh—discovered documents between them concerning potential real estate transactions."

My drink wasn't so tasty anymore. "I don't get why you think my husband was involved with those two. And lots of people are named Volkman."

"Not all of them were married to someone named Ella." Dave glanced at a man chatting with an older woman at the bar, listening patiently to his harangue. All the other customers were braving a chilly evening on the bar's patio. Dave said between his teeth, "You saw how run-down part of Pine Glen is. I think, although I have no proof, someone was letting that area deteriorate so a developer could buy it cheaply. In fact, a consortium did want to buy it. A man in Falk's running group gave me copies of letters exchanged between Falk and your husband. They included names of investors interested in the lots around and including the trash burner, like Falk. He—or they—hired Volkman's firm to arrange the deal, but it fell through. I don't know why. That's how Volkman connected with them."

"Who is this man with the copies of letters to or from Volkman?" I wiped my hands on my slacks. "Or can't I ask?"

Dave leaned across the table toward me. "Oh, come on, Ella. You know I can't tell you that. I can say he used to be a lawyer. He's a dead real estate lawyer now."

Nausea gripped my gut, and I pushed the Guinness away. "You mean, he . . . the one found in the trash burner?"

Dave just looked at me, his mouth a grim, tight line.

"I need to walk or something. Can we go?" I put a twenty on the table. Dave handed it back to me.

"I paid already. But sure. Let's walk around the neighborhood. It's trendy."

Once outside, the cool air soothed my nerves. We walked south into former railroad yards, now a residential area bustling with young families, professional types, shops, and even a cute little corner market. The place was still open.

"Let's try it," I said. "I read they make good sandwiches to go."

We walked in, ordered, and left—each of us with a baguette filled with butter, cheese, radishes, and, for Dave, a few slices of ham. Across the street, we wandered into a development of town houses and mid-rises surrounding a small city park. Finding an unoccupied bench, we sat, ate, and finally resumed our conversation. I don't know how I had an appetite. Maybe it was the fresh air. Maybe, just maybe, I liked being with Dave. What I didn't like was how much more he knew about Randy than I did.

Eating slowed my pulse. I asked Dave to explain the connection between Falk and Randy Volkman.

"I can't say. I was hoping you knew something about it, but—"

"But I don't. Not a thing."

I paused and glanced at Dave. He was biting into his sandwich and nodding. I needed to explain. "A mutual friend of our parents fixed us up. We were just friends at first, then started dating seriously. We married after a year or so. Our son was born and we moved to the suburbs. My husband embraced the new fitness craze and began running. I didn't. Wasn't my thing. I mean, I liked to *walk* long distances and in interesting places. We drifted apart. I'm not sure about the day that happened, but I realized, maybe when our son was in school and I wasn't working yet, that this married couple wasn't spending much time together."

"Uh-huh. Must have been hard on you—and your son?"

"Well, my husband was the family hero. He brought the kid into the city on what they called their adventures, 'father-son bonding.' Sometimes they were gone for a whole weekend." What *was* I doing during those quiet afternoons and nights, without Lonnie's giggles and Randy's muted voice on endless phone calls with clients?

Was Dave reading my mind? He said, "After Clarice died, I couldn't stand the silence in our place. I even missed her struggled breathing at the end." He crumpled his sandwich wrapper and stuffed it into the carry-out box.

"How did you meet?" I did not want to talk anymore about Randy, whose distanced behavior I was beginning to question with some suspicion.

"Clarice—a beautiful and smart person, one of the smartest I've ever known—went to Mount Holyoke College, a women's college in Massachusetts. She graduated with honors, Phi Beta Kappa—"

"Her major?"

"Natural science and mathematics. She was an applied mathematician."

"You went to Amherst. That's in Massachusetts, too. Is that where you met?"

"No, actually, in Chicago. She was working downtown as an actuary. It was Evan—you know, Evan Ferguson—who knew her. I forget how, but he introduced us at a friend's party. Evan was my friend in college, a poli sci major, but—Lord, what an idealist—he joined the police force. We decided to do a police leadership program together. I didn't finish. Sidetracked by, say, more pressing issues."

"Wow. I didn't, I mean . . . losing Clarice, and now Ferg . . . Evan."

Dave was staring across the park. After too long a minute he glanced at my empty take-out box. "Finished with that? Good. Let's go."

We walked in silence to the subway station and took the train back to our neighborhood. My mentioning Clarice—and Ferguson—shut Dave down. Back home, however, as I grabbed the banister to go up, he tapped the back of my hand and said, "I enjoyed this evening. You're good company, Ella. We've both lost people important to us, of course in different ways. My advice: don't dwell on the past." He waved his hand as if to brush away the last thought. "Let me know if you need anything. 'Night."

I nodded and said, "Good night." Home again, door closed, I put down my keys. My eyes were burning. After using the bathroom, I splashed my face with cold water. Toweling off, I looked hard at my reflection: shallow eye pouches cold water couldn't shrink, some new little sags around the mouth. Otherwise, not too bad. My hair was still good, dark gray streaked with white, but thick enough to style into a bouncy bob. I laughed: "bouncy" like my personality.

Then I remembered my arrangement with Lonnie for the next day, but also the doubts I was having about him and Dave. I had to know what Lonnie was doing that very evening. Pulling on a dark cap, I tucked in my hair, changed into black jeans, and slipped on a barn coat to match. I was going to Pine Glen. Whatever Lonnie was doing, I'd be in the shadows watching him until I needed the bathroom again. Really. I tiptoed down the back stairs to the side yard and slid like a ninja's shadow across the street, then turned into the alley toward Lonnie's house.

~

The wind came up. Trash bins swayed in the gusts and their shadows shifted on and off the alley's brick walls like freezing commuters waiting for their missing bus. Empty plastic bags swirled in little vortices. Dented cans clattered. I hoped the noise would cover my footsteps. Passing in back of the trash burner lot, I slipped through a tangle of bushes behind Lonnie's house until I spotted his kitchen window. I calmed myself by counting my breaths. At 120, a dim blue light came on in his kitchen. Lonnie was silhouetted against the window in and out of sight. I crouched down and resumed counting.

Someone else appeared in the window. He—or she?—was slender and moved away before I could see any details. At number 273, I felt something brush my leg. I stifled a yelp. It was the old gray cat. I grimaced and crouched to scratch her willing ears. Circling me, she collided with my legs with more force than I would imagine a cat could have, pushing me back down the alley. I lost my balance. While steadying myself, I saw movement by the trash burner.

The cat yowled as I stepped back—on her paw—to get a better view. I nudged her aside and focused on the burner lot. Whatever I had seen moments before was gone now. Intent on watching Lonnie's window, I turned back toward the house, but a noise near the burner had me swiveling too fast and, tripping over my feet, I fell to my hands and knees with a grunt. As I got up, brushing gravel and leaf debris from my jeans, I heard, "Well, look who's here. Good evening, Mrs. Castle."

Pinscher.

The kitchen window went dark. I stepped back. Pinscher followed me. "You are Mrs. Castle, right? Or may I call you Ella and ask whatever are you doing here? A little private detective work?"

"I could ask you the same thing. And no, you may not call me Ella. Simply, Mrs. Castle."

"Oh, my stars, please forgive my indiscretion." He squeezed my upper arm and snarled. "You were trespassing on city property. Move."

"I was not!"

He pushed me toward the burner lot. "I say you were, and I want some answers." I pulled away from him. If my heart were beating any higher in my chest, I'd have swallowed it. As I braced to knee Pinscher, the gray cat yowled at my side and sprang at his face. She clawed Pinscher's cheek and eye. He screeched and threw her to the ground. The cat ran down the alley. Pinscher staggered toward the street. Reaching his car, he pulled out his phone.

I saw that Lonnie's kitchen door was ajar. While Pinscher faced the street and yelled into his phone, I bolted up the stairs into the gloom.

"Hey, it's me. Mom," I whispered. "I'm sorry. Please. Help. I don't know what to do, Lonnie." I closed and locked the door. In the silent kitchen, the dim street light revealed no one. Nobody by the front door or on the stairs. I sat on the next-to-bottom step and began counting again, but my pulse hammered in my ears. I gave up. With my head on my knees, I listened for the slightest noise.

What to do? Would Pinscher arrest me? For what? My private talk with now-dead Detective Ferguson? My chance encounter with the trash burner corpses? As I shook my bewildered head, I heard footsteps on the stairs above me.

I jumped up. "Lonnie?" Shadows blanketed the treads above me. Backing toward the desk that blocked the front door, I leaned against its thick, solid side. I called out Lonnie's name again.

"Yes," he said. "And . . . and—"

"And me." A nasal voice, an old familiar nasal voice.

I waited for more. In the distance a siren honked like a maddened goose, louder as it neared Pine Glen.

"Randy?" I gagged. "How—?"

"Right," he said. The siren stopped as a car pulled up behind Pinscher's.

"Hey, get away from the window."

Ignoring this apparition of Randy, I muttered, "Who's answering Pinscher's call?" I could not turn to face my supposedly dead husband. "It's Falk!" My fingers dropped the curtain. He was scanning the house with his flashlight.

Lonnie put a hand on my shoulder and steered me toward the stairs. "Shh, Mom. Let's go upstairs. Please, try to be quiet," Lonnie whispered like a little boy with a sore throat. Randy—if it really was Randy—was gone.

"But the dog . . . I'm afraid of that dog."

Lonnie lay his hand across my mouth. It smelled like hand sanitizer. "I asked you to be quiet. Don't worry about the dog."

We climbed the creaking stairs up to a worn, wooden landing bordered by three doors shedding scabrous paint. Randy stood in front of the door to my left, his hand on the knob. "Shall we stay here or go into my room?"

"Stay here so you won't be seen or heard," Lonnie whispered.

"Is that a bathroom?" I asked, pointing my chin toward the middle door.

"If you need it. Don't flush."

I really had to go, but curiosity delayed me. A little glass brick window at the top of the stairs let in enough light from the street so that I could see Randy's face. His brown eyes were clear and bright and his hair, so thin during his illness, had thickened into a salt and pepper thatch. "Oh, Ella, I'm so tired of all this, the hiding and pretenses."

"Dad, patience. If he knocks I'll talk to him. Remember, they think you're dead." He handed me a wire coat hanger. "Mom, use this." I hung my coat on a doorknob. With a dismissive wave, I walked into the bathroom and closed the door. Time out to recalculate.

Used to the dark by now, I saw an old pull-chain toilet to my right. What I needed. After rinsing my hands under a small stream of cold water and drying with a wad of toilet paper, I remembered not to flush. On the landing, Randy was slouched against the opposite wall, hands in his pockets.

"What's going on? Am I going out of my mind? You"—I said, pointing to Randy—"you are, what, a ghost, a mirage, or a damned liar?" I caught my breath. "Both of you, damned liars! Faking your death? To do what?" I sank down to the floor and leaned against peeling wallpaper.

Lonnie was downstairs. I heard the kitchen door slam.

Before I could follow Lonnie out the door, Randy pulled me into his room. I expected icy fingers; his warm touch startled me. He pointed to the front window. "Peek through the shade," he said. "Watch what happens. They think our boy is their flunky."

Our boy. Our son. I shivered. Lonnie still called him Dad. Randy acted very much alive.

Voices echoed on the street. I peered through a hole in the ratty window shade. Without much street lighting, I could not see Lonnie's face, but his hands and shoulders said it all. He shrugged and waved his arm toward the alley and my street. Shrugging once more, he slapped his hands against his sides and turned to look down the street. Falk was growling questions as he threw the beam of his flashlight all over the burner lot. Pinscher nodded as he dabbed his face with something, probably an antiseptic wipe.

Falk spun on his heel as his beam caught the old gray cat. She streaked across the lot and escaped down the alley, Falk in pursuit. From the way he waved toward Pinscher's car, I could see Falk had ended the conversation. Pressing more wipes against his wounds, Pinscher slid behind his steering wheel and revved the motor. His car screeched away from Pine Glen. Lonnie watched them go until satisfied they were far enough away. He returned to the cottage.

"Falk will be back, you know. His car is still here."

I dropped the edge of the shade and stared at Randy. "Who are you? Why are you here in this run-down house?" My thoughts were twisting like a tangle of yarn.

"It is really me, Randy Volkman, your very much alive husband." He straightened the window shade. "Are you okay?"

"Okay?" What a stupid question. He crashed back into my life like this, and I was supposed to say, *Well a dog, the police, an unknown thief, and who knows what else attacked me, but, hey, never mind, I'm fine?* "No, I'm not okay."

Randy stepped back and muttered something like, "Not happy to see me after all."

I folded my arms across my chest. "I haven't been 'okay' for years."

"You're snarling at me."

"Like the dog that scared me to death over there." I pointed toward the trash burner.

"The dog. Well, you see—"

"Dad . . ." Lonnie said. "Not now."

Randy turned away from me and walked out of the room and downstairs.

I felt Lonnie's breath in my ear. "Mom, let's go sit. We need to explain—a lot. It's about your safety, too, now that Pinscher knows you're interested in the lot."

"Oh, he knows me alright. He spotted me at the police station. Flirted with me, would you believe?" I shuddered. "Where is that dog you were keeping?" I brushed past him and groped my way downstairs. Relieved no dog was crouching by the bottom step, I asked, "Where to now?"

Randy called from the front room. "In here."

A glow stick lay at his feet. By its blue light I saw him sprawled on a sagging dark couch. They had pushed it against the front windows whose curtains glowed faintly from the full moon. Two folding chairs bracketed a tiled coffee table. That was it, no more furniture, unless I missed something in the dark.

"That table's just like the one from our house."

"It is that one," Lonnie said. "See my initials on that leg?"

"How did—"

"Goodwill."

I nodded. I had donated most of my suburban furniture there.

Randy leaned forward. "Please, keep it down. In case Falk comes snooping around." He picked up the glow stick. "We don't need this now. Lonnie, put it in the fridge." He turned to me. "Can't put it out. No 'off' switch. Not like me. My light went out long ago."

Furious, I picked up a chair and banged it on the floor, with the table between me and Randy.

"Ella! Quiet," Randy squawked. "We're not here, remember?"

I sat down. I needed an anchor—I felt as if my body were floating away from itself. What kind of a world was this? I had moved to this block, the perfect setting for a peaceful retirement. Instead, I was in the middle of a crime novel. Words wouldn't come to me. Randy's dark form sat opposite me. His every exhale grated like sandpaper. Footsteps brought me back. Lonnie closed the kitchen door and, joining us, sat in the other chair. After a lull, while I tried to catch my breath, he said, "Mom, promise you'll listen. This is . . . complicated. No interruptions, all right?"

I nodded.

"I can't hear you. Are you okay?"

I croaked, "Don't ever ask again if I'm okay. I'm sick of that question. No, how could I be okay?" Frowning my fiercest face, I said, "Fine. Go on then. I won't talk until you're done."

"Dad, I go first?"

Randy must have agreed because Lonnie cleared his throat and began. "You know I never worked in London. I was always here."

I almost said, "In this awful place. You could have called me." But I didn't.

He went on. "Obviously, Dad didn't die. Well, not in the usual way." I stood up, but Lonnie's scowl was like a big hand pushing me back to my seat. "He needed help, and I was there for him. I hid him here and in the apartment next to you. He—" Heavy footsteps on the back porch. I jumped out of my chair when someone pounded on the door.

~

"Falk. He's back. Upstairs—both of you. Now." Lonnie was stripping off his hoodie. "Go on."

Randy locked his hand around my wrist and pulled me upstairs. I tripped on an uneven tread before we reached the landing. He grabbed my elbow and pulled me into his room. Closing the door he leaned against it, one ear on the wood panel. "Lonnie's making like Falk just woke him up, like he was sleeping on the couch." Waving me toward the bed, he whispered, "Sit, sit," and turned away. I pushed him aside and put my own ear to the door.

Lonnie was yelling. "Why the hell are you bothering me? I get too little sleep anyway what with my job. Stop poking me in the chest."

Falk said, "That Ella woman was snooping around. You'd better do something about it if you know what's good for you."

Lonnie faked a laugh. "Anyway, the murders'll scare her away. She won't be back. Not to worry. I'll make up a story about unit 2A."

I spun Randy around by his shoulder. I mouthed, "What's with 2A?" Randy waved me down with two hands and whispered that he'd explain after Falk left. I wanted to race downstairs and throttle Falk for threatening my son. The veins in my temples were humming.

Randy grasped my upper arms and whispered, "Slow down. Deep breath. I promise you the truth."

I stared at him, this man I had married but hardly knew. He stood bigger, more muscular than I remembered him. Cut, really. His black T-shirt skimmed his body and outlined his muscles. He hardly resembled the sickly puddle of apathy he used to be. He caught my expression and half-smiled.

"You seem a lot healthier than you did the day you disappeared. What are you eating?" I whispered.

I could hardly hear his answer. "Meat. Red meat. I could go for a steak right now if . . ."

"If you weren't hiding." A slammed door cut our hushed exchange. We both leaned against the door and waited for Lonnie to call us. Instead, I heard him pacing between the kitchen and front room. Randy waved me back and jerked open the door.

"Hey, he's gone?"

"Yeah, Dad. I had to wait. He walked around the burner lot for a while, then drove off." Randy was beside him before I'd reached the bottom step. While he was talking to Lonnie too low for me to hear, he balled his fists. He was ready to launch like Superman.

I plopped into my chair in the front room and said, "Hello. I'm still waiting for an explanation." Randy joined me and leaned back into the couch.

Lonnie coughed and asked if I wanted some water. "Go on, Dad," he said as he went into the kitchen. Randy grimaced. "Ella, remember how I'd disappeared into the lake? That I'd left my clothes and wallet behind?"

"Not easy to forget."

"Lonnie was with me, helped me set it up."

"What? Police said they traced footprints heading toward the water and only found a large dog's paw prints nearby."

Randy rubbed his temples. "This is the hard part." His glare hit me like two laser beams. "I was that dog." He jumped up and walked toward me. I slid off my chair and put it between us.

"Don't you get any closer to me. This is BS; people don't turn into dogs. You faked your death to get out of our marriage, didn't you? All that time I believed you, believed you were dying, and I was there for you. While Lonnie was in London and—" Glancing at the kitchen, I felt tears pooling on my lower lids. "But he wasn't. I see, he was with you. How—" I coughed away a sob. "How could you do this to me?"

"I told you. I was protecting him, and I thought you were managing." Randy scratched his head and swiped his mouth before going on. "Here's how it's been working. A land trust is the owner of this cottage, a few other houses here, and the apartment you live in. Your neighbors are renters, too."

"My lawyer never—"

"Never let on. He did try to dissuade you. These properties are in a land trust meant to protect Lonnie's interests. It's a fluke, your moving into the building on Cedargrove. Weird." He scratched his ear. "When our lawyer told us about your move, we—"

"Wait, you knew I was here? Why didn't you call me? Why all the secrecy?"

"I told you. I had to hide and I thought you were managing, because Lonnie shared your emails with me."

I took the glass of water Lonnie offered me, and he sat on the couch. Chugging his drink, Lonnie burped, then said, "It boils down to this: Dad was setting up a deal with a developer. He even—uh—was associated with some of the properties the guy wanted, but when Dad found out the guy was a crook he quashed the deal. The development would have ruined the neighborhood. As I said, the developer cursed him, and Dad sickened. They wanted to kill him."

"Ridiculous. People don't die from curses. Doctor Lawlor said Randy had a rare incurable disease. They didn't even have a name for it."

Lonnie leaned forward, his glass drained. "What I said: they didn't have a name for it because a curse was killing him."

I pressed my palms into the chair back until they hurt. This was real. I paced around the room. Every time Randy or Lonnie started to speak, I waved them off and told them roughly to stop talking. I had to think. Then I remembered what Dave had said about Falk and Pinscher knowing Randy.

I stopped pacing. "You two," I said. "Are you partners with Falk and Pinscher? Who owns the trash burner lot? No, Randy, sit down. Now." He glared at me for a moment, then shrugged. That's when I nearly stopped breathing. "Are you the trash burner killer dog?"

⁓

As morning light brightened the curtains, I stretched in my chair and rubbed my aching neck. Answering my accusations the previous night, Randy had insisted he had never hurt anyone since he'd begun to shift. As a dog he stayed close to Lonnie and guarded the cottage when Lonnie was away. He'd meant to scare me when I first spotted him, but hearing Mozart reminded him of family and his humanity. Quashing guard dog instincts, he had turned away from me and hid in the burner while he shifted to his human form. And, by the way, no corpse was in the burner then.

I found Lonnie snoring on the couch. Randy wasn't with him, nor in the kitchen. I called Randy, but he didn't answer. The patter of paws on the stairs raised the hair on the back of my neck. The dog stopped on the bottom step. He lowered his black and white spotted head, then stepped one paw at a time to the floor. Settling in like a sphinx, he cocked his head to the side.

"Randy?"

He rested his head on his paws and blinked at me. I felt a hand on my shoulder. Lonnie patted my back and said, "Mom, meet Daytime Dad."

I was riding a merry-go-round that wouldn't stop. How could my mortal, biped husband be a quadruped canine? I had seen his strength wither and had wondered how he'd made it to that beach. But here he was, a sturdy, watchful, and self-aware dog. I turned away from him, an inch at a time, and faced Lonnie. My son was leaning on the desk pushed against the front door. "Lonnie, you're both asking me to accept the impossible. Randy could be upstairs now, hiding wherever you stowed the dog before. He swore he wasn't the killer, but how can I trust his word?"

He walked into the kitchen. Pulling back the window covering, he pointed to the trash burner. "You have to. The murders look like they happened there. Who knows if the victims died elsewhere, and the murderer or murderers put the corpses there later? The city owns that lot, and the, the whatchamacallit, the trust manages this one, the two east of us, and three across the street. They're the properties the developer wanted. Somehow, he was going to get the trash burner lot from the city."

"Dave told me Falk and Pinscher were involved somehow with that deal. Ferguson's corpse . . . I mean, how weird was it that he was killed right after I talked with him outside the station? Ferguson—such a nice man." I was babbling and shivering again. "Oh, I can't stomach this. Is it cold in here? I don't feel so well."

"Who told you about Dad's involvement?"

"Straybill."

"You shouldn't be talking to him."

"But—"

"No buts. And you need something to eat," Lonnie said as he rummaged in the kitchen cabinet and pulled out some ramen packages. "I know, too salty, but it will help." He filled an electric kettle and took out two bowls. Once the ramen was ready, we brought our bowls into the living room. The dog followed us. Lonnie poured some kibble into a big metal dish, and I watched "Randy" gobble it like an ordinary dog. Nausea set in and, putting my bowl on the coffee table, I mimed an imminent barf.

"Upstairs, to your left, next to the big bedroom."

"No thanks, it's all just too much. I'll be fine. The idea that Randy . . ." I looked at the dog licking his bowl. I sat again, twisted my fork into the noodles, and, with my first mouthful, my nausea vanished. I wolfed down the rest. After rinsing the bowl in the kitchen sink, I dried it with paper towels, and returned to the living room. The dog was lying on his side and sleeping.

"So, my neighbor Dave is an undercover police detective—"

"Yeah? Maybe so." He drained his bowl. "I mean, you said he knew about the developer's plans? I don't trust him." The dog woke up and growled.

"Calm down, Lonnie—*and* Randy," I said. "Dave isn't the problem. What I wanted to say was that he thinks he knows who else might be involved in the trash burner murders. Dave learned that one of the victims, killed around the time of Randy's death, was a Loop lawyer, a big name, but he didn't tell me who it was."

The dog barked twice. Lonnie answered, "Yeah, Dad. It was Rothman, the real estate lawyer. The one who told you to nix the deal." I swear the dog nodded, then lowered his head onto his forelegs and closed his eyes.

"Getting close to this Dave guy, Mom?" The dog's head popped up and he stared at me.

"No, we're just neighbors and talk to each other. He was with me, though, when we found Ferguson's body in the trash burner."

"How convenient."

"What are you implying? Dave was his friend. He was sick about it."

Lonnie stabbed at his last noodles. "Sure, sure."

How perfect it was that I'd just eaten noodles. They mirrored my state of mind. Randy was somehow involved with this cottage and a bunch of other properties, including my place on Cedargrove. Now they were in a trust set up so Lonnie could live there. Falk and Pinscher and some developer wanted the properties badly enough to be suspected of murdering whoever got in their way. Sitting in my chair again, I gazed at the sleeping dog for a while. He looked relaxed and carefree. Then I saw Lonnie. He was on the couch and staring at me while munching potato chips one by one.

"How did the curse work?" I asked, nearly in a whisper.

❧

Lonnie sat next to me on the couch as he booted up a laptop. "This is Dad's," he said. The dog bolted awake and whined. In a few moments, desktop icons appeared on the screen. He clicked on Randy's browser. A bold red circle popped up with a line crossing it and the words, *STOP! Unauthorized site.*

"Well, that's that?"

"No, that's good. We don't want it to work. When Dad wouldn't cooperate with the developer and his cronies, they hacked his laptop to threaten him. They carried out the threat."

"How?"

"They said he'd be sorry, and he would lose everything dear to him."

"Wait, did 'dear' include us? Do 'they'—I assume Falk and Pinscher—know what we look like?"

"Yeah, they knew all about you from the photo Dad had in his wallet. Also my eighth-grade graduation photo—but they don't know what I look like today. I'm Joe to them. They think I'm renting from a land trust, too, like you."

"So, that's how Pinscher recognized me." I stared at the dog. "Did Randy fight back?"

"He decided to report them to some authority, like the Triple B or whatever. I can't remember. He worked at it, for a few days. Then, his browser began to stutter. It dropped letters for a while, then typed in weird text he'd never entered. He thought he was going crazy."

"Was he?"

"No, but that's when he started to lose weight, couldn't hold down his food—you know, all those mysterious symptoms the doctors couldn't fix. Meanwhile, the glitches stopped, but every once in a while the screen would flash an image that went by too fast to catch. That's when he really began to fade."

"And spend all his time on the couch."

"Right. Maybe you didn't notice, but I snuck in one day when you were out and borrowed his computer. I brought it here, plugged it in, and opened the browser. I typed in any old thing, just to see what would happen. In the middle of my nonsense sentence, a woman's face popped up, live—well, not her real face but an avatar. You know, an AI face. She started talking to me, like, 'Keep Randy away from this device' and a dialogue box appeared saying, 'Click here to connect with me.' I thought *I* was going crazy, but nothing made sense anymore, so I did connect with her."

"What was she like? Young, old, pretty?"

"Older, nothing special about her. The avatar had gray hair . . ." Lonnie stroked his chin. "I thought that was a weird choice and she had the coldest, big blue eyes with tiny pupils, almost like slits."

I thought of the gray cat, the rain, Fanny's wet hair. "Like Fanny Katzer?"

Lonnie grabbed the computer as it started to slide off his lap. He rubbed his eyes and stared at me. Shaking his head, he said with a crooked smile, "How could I have missed that? Yes, I'm joking. I did find out she was Fanny."

"But she claims she hardly knows you exist and wouldn't ask you to fix anything."

"Right. Right." He eyed the trash burner lot. "But she does know me. Complained about noises in 2A one day. What's more important is that once we connected online, in public she claimed to have no use for me, but in private she told me she knew a way to fight the curse. Then she gave me a plan. After a few days, her message was on Dad's screen. She said her hack was working, and I should taxi Dad to the lakeshore. You know the rest. She changed the curse. The sickness is gone, but, trouble is, he's stuck in Fanny's dog disguise. During the day he's a dog but at sundown he's Dad. He has to hide at night. I tried keeping him in 2A, but it was too risky, so he lives here now and, well, we're stuck here. Unless we can find some way to get Falk and Pinscher off our backs."

"Could Dave Straybill help?"

"Too risky. How do we know we can trust him?"

"I'll find out." I stood up, put an arm around my son's shoulders, and squeezed him lightly. Lonnie pressed my hand against his cheek. "Watch your back, Mom. We don't know who to trust these days—except maybe Fanny."

Trust? Definitely not Pinscher or Falk, my two possibly mortal enemies now. Would Dave help me? The dog was staring at me. He tilted his head, mouth open, and tongue hanging out as if he were grinning. I felt like saying "good dog," but turned from him and, waving to Lonnie, went out the back door. No one was around. I stepped into the alley, but stopped to call Dave on my cell phone.

I heard his voice mail message. "Hi. Straybill here. Not available right now. At the tone, leave your message and a callback number." I did just that. My message was short, simply asking him to call me ASAP. For emphasis or in case he didn't listen to voicemail, I texted him the same message.

Now what? I wasn't thrilled about going back to my building in case Pinscher was waiting there. I felt my stomach clutch at the thought and decided to sneak in by the back door. What if Dave didn't call back? How to go home safely? Definitely not down that alley. Approaching the corner of Pine Glen and Cedargrove, I walked behind the school and followed the alley behind it. I passed a few bungalows, came to a driveway, and crossed the street. Turning into the alley behind our building, I hoped long morning shadows would hide me.

Something soft bumped my left calf. I glanced down. The gray cat. "Fanny?" I said on impulse. The cat meowed and dashed into the yard. She reached the bottom step of our building and looked as if she wanted me to follow, which of course I did. She head-butted the back door and trotted past Fanny's apartment door, also ajar. I followed her inside. She pawed the door closed and ran into the bedroom alcove. Sky-blue curtains covered the sliding glass door.

I decided to wait on the cushiony sofa for her next move. As I took in Fanny's place, my phone vibrated. "Hello?"

"Hey, it's Dave."

"Hi. Where are you? Home?"

"No, I'm meeting with . . . somebody right now. I'll be back this afternoon. You sounded pretty upset. What's up? Did you learn something new?"

Who was Dave meeting? And now he was asking *me* for information. Maybe I couldn't trust him after all? "No, nothing to report. I just called to see if you were okay. If any of those guys were bothering you. Oh, by the way, I sort of ran into Pinscher last night."

"Where? Why?"

"It's not that important," I lied. "He's got some kind of animus against me. Can't figure it out. Anyway, how about meeting again for a drink? We can talk then."

"Sure, but I don't like this Pinscher thing. Be careful. Let's go back to Caitlin's, okay? Say about five thirty?"

"Excellent. Good choice. See you there." I hung up, more confused than ever. I wanted to see Dave, not only because he was attractive and attentive, but also to see how honest he was. Recent singularities were draining my faith in humanity and the term "normal" . . . I just didn't know whom to trust anymore.

Fanny—the human Fanny—was standing inside the frame of the bedroom alcove. Her blue oversized shirt matched her eyes. She paired it with soft gray slacks. Barefoot, she walked into the kitchen, saying, "You sure are taking a lot of chances, Ella. Those cops could have killed you last night." She switched on the electric kettle. "I'm making us some mint tea. You're guessing mine is catnip, a close relative of mint." She laughed and took out two mugs from the kitchen cabinet over her sink.

"Fanny, I don't understand any of this, especially the cat and dog story." I opened my right hand and indicated her place, my place upstairs, then pointed to the street. "I mean, I know you know about Lonnie and Randy. You've been kind to me, but not up front."

"You're right. I haven't been honest with you, but you stumbled into this situation, and we didn't want you to get hurt."

"*We?*"

Fanny sat on the edge of the sofa and, leaning into her steaming mug for a few thoughtful sips, said, "I meant the royal 'we.' You know, me, myself, and I—except there is no third Fanny. Only what you've seen or guessed at." She stretched the kinks out of her neck and, tucking her legs under her, nestled into the sofa's cushions. "I suppose you want an explanation."

"I've been hearing a lot of explanations lately. So, yes. Are you really a catwoman, like in the comics? What connection do you have to Randy and Lonnie? Why did you pretend not to know who I was and why—"

"Please, please listen to this. First of all, I'm not a comic book heroine, but I am a shifter."

Thinking this situation was unreal, that I was living in some paranormal fantasy novel, I shook my head and muttered, "Oh, come on. Randy's curse and supposed life as a dog has been too weird to believe. Now, you say you're a . . . a what?"

"A shape-shifter. Someone who switches between his or her human form and that of an animal, usually because of magic, inheritance, or a curse." Her unblinking blue eyes caught my surprise.

"You mean, like a werewolf or the Greek god Zeus who became a swan, a bull, or a cuckoo, depending on the girl he lusted after? This is too much, Fanny. It happens in fairy tales and myths, not on Cedargrove in the heart of the city. The real problem here is my safety. Falk is after me, I'm sure."

"He's such a sh—so shameful," she hissed. "Anyway, believe me, my shifting is real. I inherited my ability to transform physically whenever I want, and strictly as that cat. Randy can't control his changes—a dog in the day, his human form sunset to sunrise. A very modern digitally transmitted spell sickened him. I helped modify Randy's curse, but until the person who requested the curse dies, Randy will shift. Oh, and if you wondered why I intervened . . . ? Lonnie, aka Joe, and I talked." She looked into her mug as she said, "Knowing some curses and cures myself, I decided to help. Also, anything to fight that Animal Control Officer."

That was the clearest explanation I'd heard all day and it was consistent with Lonnie's account. Fanny sipped more of her tea and her eyes closed halfway. From what I knew about cats, she was signaling she liked me. In that moment, I believed in Randy's story, if not in my own sanity, but what would be my next step? I told Fanny I was going to meet Dave at 5:30 that evening. She leaped up from the sofa, tea mug balanced perfectly in one hand.

"You're what?"

"Meeting Dave Straybill at Caitlin's, just to ask him a few more questions about the cold case file he mentioned to me, the one about the trash burner murders. He's investigated those cases. Hey, from the way you cared for him after the attack, I thought you'd mellowed toward him."

"How did you know he was—"

"A detective? He told me. He knows I'm Ella Volkman, but he thinks Randy is dead."

She brought her mug to the kitchen sink, then turned quickly and leaped onto the counter. The strong morning sun spotlighted her as she glared at me and said, "Keep it that way. Learn as much as you can but don't share what you know. He's going to wonder about your meeting Pinscher at night. Use the story about my—the cat—rescuing you to distract him from any questions about Lonnie and the cottage." She jumped to the floor.

"Fanny, how'd you do that? At your age—I mean, I couldn't."

"My cat nature. And I'm anciently young," she smirked. "Fine. Have a good evening." She stared deep into my eyes. "I know you like Dave, but keep your eye on him. Be discreet." She opened the door and bowed while swinging her hand toward the hallway. I wanted to hug her as possibly the only character in my story I could believe in, but she swept me into the hallway and closed her door.

As I walked upstairs, my stomach growled. Since all I'd eaten over nearly 24 hours was a cup of ramen, I made straight for my kitchen, heated up a leftover wedge of pizza for lunch, and poured myself a goblet of Chianti. Kicking off my shoes, I settled in the armchair, put up my feet, and opened my newest *New Yorker*. Alternating warm, tomatoey bites of pizza with sips of wine, I skimmed through articles. I froze at seeing a drawing on page 46. It was one of the funny, often weird cartoons punctuating the magazine. Two people were sitting at a restaurant table. One had a cat's head and the other a dog's. The caption had to do with two menus, the only objects on the table—something about not being able to read—but it punctured my relaxation bubble. How did the cartoon editor know I was in the middle of a shapeshifter saga? I didn't need any reminders. I dropped the magazine on the floor, finished the pizza wedge, and leaned back to sip at my wine.

More than three hours later, I woke up, still in the armchair. The empty wine glass was on my side table, sitting next to the magazine I'd dropped on the floor. Somewhat shaky, I got up and checked the door, just in case. Still locked. Walking over to the windows, I saw one was slightly ajar, but the screen was in place and the windowsill's dust was undisturbed. It had become cloudy outside and rain was in the forecast. I shut the window and locked it.

Convinced I'd tidied up in a daze before zonking out, I went to the bathroom, put my Ninja outfit in the hamper, and searched my closet for something else to wear. Pairing a long brown and black sweater with black leggings and ankle boots would do, I thought, especially accented by my private-eye style trench coat. I was looking forward to seeing Dave. Perhaps we could be friends, especially since we both had known rough times. Maybe this rendezvous would lead to fun for me and release for Randy from his curse.

~

Caitlin's was buzzing by 5:15 when I arrived. Sidewalk tables, still out in the autumn chill, were packed with thirty-somethings laughing and chatting over their beers, despite rain in the forecast. Portable heaters cast a rosy glow over the tables. Inside at the bar, no stool lacked a customer. Nearly every table was occupied. Then, I spotted a two-top in a gloomy back corner of the room, near a wall of refrigerated drinks and snacks. I draped my trench coat over the chair opposite me and waited for Dave.

"Hey, Mrs. Volkman. What a coincidence. Have you been following me?"

My breath caught in my throat. Pinscher! I eyed him without answering until he asked if he could join me. He had a patch over one eye and red claw marks on the cheek underneath. "No! And you're still mistaken. I'm Mrs. Castle and I'm expecting a friend."

"A *friend*? Well, your friends are my friends." His grin faded. "More than you know."

I refused to answer him. Watching the front door, I saw Dave arrive. He noticed Pinscher hovering over me. He waved and put his finger to his lips. I half-heard Pinscher asking me about my late night visit to the trash burner. I would have said I was only looking for my lost and obviously protective cat, but Dave strolled over, beer in hand.

"Well, look who's here. Detective Pinscher, right? Hey, man, what happened to your face?"

Pinscher straightened up and looked around the room. Clearing his throat, which made the Adam's apple in his scrawny neck bounce, he said, "Just a little problem with a cat." Sneering, he turned to Dave. "So, Straybill. You've been away for a while, right? Why was that? Oh yeah, some kind of manslaughter charge?" He looked at me and rolled his eyes.

"Let me update you," said Dave. "They dropped the charge. I've been on special assignments since then. Sorry about your accident. Anyway, this is my neighbor, Ella. You know her?"

I interrupted. "No, but he thinks he does. He's been following me. Really rude."

Pinscher snorted. "Sorry, ma'am. We met a few days ago. Just being friendly. Normally, I wouldn't waste my time," he said before leaving the bar.

I watched him go. Dave examined his drink.

I said, "I don't get it. He followed me here. I'm sure of it."

"Probably not. More likely you had an accidental meeting. He lives down the block—er, according to my records. But we're here to talk about Falk *and* Pinscher, right? By the way, he's wrong. You aren't wasting anyone's time, especially mine. May I move your coat and sit?"

Through the plate glass front window, I saw Pinscher chatting with a couple of men seated on the terrace. One of them looked familiar but I couldn't place him. Pinscher pointed with an open hand to the interior and the three of them laughed. I smiled at Dave and moved my coat. Without sitting, he asked, "A Guinness?"

"You remembered. Yes, thanks, a pulled one, please."

By the time we both had our drinks, Pinscher had left. I slumped into my chair, trench coat cushioning my back. "Hey, thanks again." I sighed. "Pinscher . . . what's his problem?"

"He just wanted to say hello and you were ungrateful?"

"No. Rather, he scares me a bit. Last night, I was searching for the gray cat, you know, the one that hangs around our building. I've been making friends with her. She's feral, but I'm trying to tame her, you could say—so, I was hunting for her in the alley across the street and then down behind Pine Glen. Pinscher must have been hanging around the trash burner, I guess, because he surprised me. Grabbed my arm, pulled me into the lot, and said he was going to ask me some questions. But the cat appeared and jumped at his face. He was screaming as I ran away. And that's why he has a bandage on his face."

"I don't know what cat you're talking about, but

you think Pinscher wants something from you?"

"Well, maybe. I wonder why he was in that lot at night."

Dave played with his beer. "Don't know." After a few handfuls of popcorn, he said, "I've uncovered some information that might interest you, more about Falk and Pinscher, but first I'm curious. When did your husband get sick?"

I wanted to tell Dave enough to interest him but nothing to endanger my family more. "We'd been married for less than twenty years when his symptoms appeared and slowly worsened."

"And how long ago did he die?"

"A few years ago. I've lost track of time. We married when I was young."

"You're fifty-seven now, right?"

I sighed and squinted. "How did you know? And why should you care?"

He said, "My investigation touched on you, too. Sorry. I'm fifty-eight. Clarice died at fifty-two, but I feel like it was yesterday."

Dave was reaching out, in a way—two spouses dead from illness, a widow and widower alone in the world, yadda, yadda, yadda—yet after I told him I truly sympathized I added, "Well, you're part of *my* investigation. I mean, with all the weird stuff that's been going on, I'd like to know if you've learned anything new." After a beat, I said, "And what's that about a manslaughter charge?" Was Pinscher trying to gaslight me about Dave?

"Let's get that last one out of the way. I'll make it simple. My partner and I were pursuing a stolen car. It was winter. Black ice covered the road. We were all going too fast. The perp's car spun, hit our car, then skidded off the road, over the embankment. It flipped several times. The driver was dead. My partner was driving our squad car. Sustained a head injury. I had a few cuts but was otherwise fine. The dead man's family brought charges, but the case was dismissed."

"Makes sense. Sorry, that must have been awful. But getting back to the trash burner business . . ."

"Oh . . . right. I did find out that the first of the so-called trash burner victims was a guy named Cedric Rothman. A real estate lawyer with a downtown practice. Your husband had a business relationship with him."

"Rothman . . . Rothman. I never heard Randy mention him before or during his illness." That was close to the truth. "How did they know each other?"

"I have some documents between Rothman and Volkman—I mean, Randy—that discussed the pros and cons of selling certain properties that Randy either owned or represented, I'm not sure which."

"What properties?" My armpits were starting to feel damp.

"Don't know. They didn't say." He leaned toward me. "Confidentially, it sounded familiar. The NIMBY argument."

"NIMBY?"

"Not In My Back Yard. Apparently the project would have leveled a lot of vintage homes, especially some middle-income family homes and two-flats that fed kids into the neighborhood school. The documents noted a few families had heard about the project, threatened to sue, but sold out in the end."

"To whom?"

"A dummy corporation . . ." Dave paused and stared at me. "Headed by Falk—" He paused. "Oh, and somehow Pinscher was involved." He sat back with a fat grin on his face. "But our building and a number of others on Pine Glen, like the cottage next to the trash burner lot, are not part of that."

I stared back at him and didn't answer. Sipping at my Guinness, I scanned the bar. "Pinscher has been harassing me ever since I met with Ferguson at the district police station. Falk has been consistently rude to me, too, especially after we found the first body in the trash burner. So, now I'm thinking—"

"You're thinking Pinscher and Falk suspect you know who owns the properties they want and could be persuaded—not so nicely—to sell them if you were actually the owner?"

"Well, possibly, except I don't know anything," I lied. "Pinscher is nasty and would have arrested me last night, regardless of my cat story, just for trespassing or whatever, if Fa—" I faked a giggle. "Sorry. The Guinness is getting to me. I was saying if my cat friend hadn't given me a chance to run away. As you saw, Pinscher is totally unrepentant."

"He is such a pu—I mean, nasty, as you say. And you might be right, but you don't own any of those rundown lots or the building, do you?"

"Oh, come on. No, I'm just a tenant. I pay online monthly to that land trust, uh, Fifteen Fifteen Trust LLC, I think. Don't you?"

"Yep, my landlord, too." He finished his beer and raised his glass. "Would you like another?"

"No, thanks. I'm getting hungry."

He pushed back his chair and stood up. "I know a great little Mexican restaurant just down the street."

"I'd rather not stay around here. You can understand why. Anyway, I'll just use the ladies' before going home."

"Right, King is probably wondering where I am. It's *his* dinner time too. I'll meet you outside."

When I left the bar, Dave was talking to two bald or closely shaven men seated at one of the terrace tables, both dressed in running gear. They were the men Pinscher had chatted with earlier. Close up, I recognized one, from Falk's running group. Dave saw me, turned quickly from them with a wave, and grabbed my elbow.

I yanked my arm from his grip. "That wasn't necessary. I would not have interrupted your conversation. Who were they, anyway?"

Dave studied my face and shrugged. "Two guys in the department. They think I'm on a date. I did not want to get into introductions."

"Oh, it's a team thing. Why not introduce me?"

"They know I'm a private guy."

"I thought you were a private eye."

"Ha! As long as they think we're seeing each other, why don't we? I mean, let's have dinner somewhere, my treat."

"What about King?"

"He's the king of kibble. He'll be fine."

I smiled. "I assumed he would miss you."

"King? No, he's probably happy to have alone time."

"Okay, then. Let's go." An actual dinner date. I couldn't resist.

∼

We ate at Ristorante Mar e Mannu, a place Dave knew, only a few blocks from home, but I'd never noticed it before. Its Sardinian menu included fregola—a round Sardinian pasta—with mussels that I enjoyed. Dave had tuna with vegetables. We chatted about everything but the "case."

I excused myself to use the restroom and when I returned, a bowl of coffee gelato was waiting for me. My favorite. "Aren't you having any, Dave? I don't like eating dessert alone."

He patted his belly. "Been putting on a few pounds lately, so, go on. Enjoy."

Afterwards, we strolled back to our building. Dave scanned the property with his pocket flashlight several times before we went inside. He saw me to my door and, before leaving, asked me to look around and let him know if everything was all right.

"Why don't you come in and see for yourself?" I said with a wink. With a face as grim as an undertaker's, he looked around. After beaming his flashlight through one of my windows, I assumed to check the street, he said, "Looks good. Lock your windows, especially the balcony doors. Call me tomorrow around nine, okay?" With that, he shook my hand, as if to reassure me all would be well, and went down to his apartment. His handshake left a gummy residue on my palm. *Oh, guys*, I thought. *Use a table napkin.*

~

I slept well that night—or thought I did, but in the morning, before I opened my eyes, I couldn't move my arms or legs. *What was in that gelato,* I mused before panicking.

Rough hands pulled me forward. I wasn't in bed, but perched on the edge of a chair in a big, darkened room. Before I could see more, someone covered my eyes with a scratchy cloth and tied it tightly behind my head. Panic definitely gripped me at that moment. I could hardly breathe. A muffled voice said, "Carson, she's awake. Hey, don't tape her mouth. She'll have to answer his questions."

His? *Carson*? I thought, holding my breath in panic. *If I'm hearing names, I'm not going to survive this.*

The room was cold, and I shivered, wearing no more than my flannel cat pajamas. I ignored my full bladder as confusion took over. How did they invade my place? Doors and windows were locked. I regretted not installing a chain right after moving in.

"She'll scream," said the other male voice, raspy and higher.

"If she does, no one will hear her."

They laughed. "We better check in with, you know, him. She's not going anywhere anyhow."

I couldn't speak anyway, not a peep. My teeth were chattering as I shivered in the dark. Carson had been one of the men tending to Ferguson's corpse. He and the other man had abducted me for someone else. Who else but Pinscher?

How had I slept through being abducted, and where in the hell was I? Sudden nausea made me wonder if I'd been drugged. Before going to bed, I had felt gentle weariness sweep over me as I finished brushing my teeth. By the time I was in my jammies and under the covers, I was gone.

A door clicked and I heard a bolt-lock slide and slam into place. "Hey, come back!" I tried to yell, then, clearing my dry throat, I croaked, "Who are you? What do you want?" No one answered. I heard an engine start up and car tires squeal.

At Caitlin's, Pinscher had harassed me, and before that he had threatened me with arrest by the trash burner. Neither voice of my captors matched his, but he certainly would have plenty of time to interrogate me here later. Still groggy from whatever knocked me out, I moaned as my abduction sank in; someone wanted me out of the way, yet right then I was alive and unhurt. One of the kidnappers mentioned tape. Like a TV crime show victim, I felt something binding my legs and wrists. My arms were in my lap, not behind the chair back. Careless. Although my wrists were taped, my fingers were free. I pushed the blindfold over my forehead.

After blinking my eyes into focus, I looked around my prison, a bare, gloomy room, like a concrete garage or storeroom. A heap of clothes or rags lay against a wall deep in shadow. A folding table leaned against another wall. Dim daylight seeped through the room's one dust-streaked clerestory window, higher than my head. It shared the wall with a wide metal door. What was outside? My snatchers had forgotten to tie me to the chair. Were they incompetent, or did they leave me like that deliberately? I stood up. My legs gave out and I fell to the floor. My right elbow and knee hit the concrete first. Pain jolted my funny bone, and a broad, stinging wound was spreading across my knee.

I struggled to rise. Rolling onto my stomach, I pressed my elbows into the floor. Fiery needles shot up my arm to my neck. Taking a deep breath, I pushed through the pain until I was on my knees. I shuffled back to the chair. Leaning on it, I pulled my legs forward and stood. Gnawing the cut end of tape near my thumb, I freed my hands, then unwrapped my legs and shook them out. Tingling at first, my toes and then my calves sprang to life—plus a sharp pain in my knee.

At last, I could relieve myself. Stiff and aching from hip to toe, I hobbled to a corner of the room, stripped off my bottoms, and let go. Old newspaper and homework papers littered the floor. Handy for toilet paper, but I used the blindfold. My pajama bottoms were a mess. Stains weren't as bad as the shredded cloth around my scraped knee. A bruise was forming on my elbow, too, but nothing felt broken.

My stomach growled. Breakfast time had long passed, although the window still framed daylight. Eager to look out, I pulled the chair to the wall, led with my good leg, and grabbed the concrete sill. Grime obscured my view. I spit on the lowest part of the window pane and used my sleeve to clean it.

My *prison* was part of a large L-shaped building with a broad but empty parking lot behind it. Across an alley, several bungalows faced the lot. The sun was on the other side of the building I was in; perhaps it was afternoon. Clouds were gathering, adding to the bleak scene of one-car garages and trash cans across the way.

The alley looked like hundreds of alleys in my town, but this one jogged a memory. Stealing home from Lonnie's the previous day, I had scooted along an alley just like that one. Then it hit me; I was in the back of the school at the intersection of Pine Glen

and Cedargrove. I was looking at the same bungalows and garages, but later in the day.

A thin crack ran from the pane I had cleared to-
wards the center of the window. I tapped it and the
part near the frame's glazing gave a little. Hoping to
find something with heft I could use to pound out the
glass, I limped around the room. In its darkest corner I found a couple of dusty backpacks. I upended
one and shook it out. A small flashlight clunked to
the floor. I pressed its switch; it was dead. I dug into
the pack's zipper pockets. No papers, no IDs, no wallet, but I did find an untouched granola bar, which I
gobbled. A bottle with some water lay at the bottom
of the other backpack. I was so thirsty I drank it all.

Energized by the granola bar and grasping the
flashlight, I mounted the chair again. Shielding
my eyes with my left arm, I pounded the window's
cracked pane, focusing on its weakest point. The
crack lengthened, but I could not shatter the glass.
Just then, an animal caught my eye as it raced across
the lot, faster than a coyote or fox on the run. It disappeared around the building's far corner. Hoping
it would return, I pounded on the window pane but
soon quit, disgusted with myself for thinking a wild
animal could help me. Feeling foolish, I stowed the
flashlight in my top's breast pocket.

I looked at the empty lot. No squirrels, no spar-
rows, not even a rat. I couldn't see the ground, but I
thought that if a dumpster were below, I could break
out the glass, jump, and run home. My mouth went

dry; I had no key, no ID, nothing. Yet surely Dave or Fanny would miss me and find me before my captors did away with me. Maybe Lonnie would risk revealing himself and come for me. But how would any of them know I was here? The questions would not stop, and my body sagged from fatigue. I peered out the window one more time.

A car drove into the lot and parked on the far side near the alley. I ducked down and sat in the chair. Were they coming back to grill me? Or was the driver simply parking there? No use sitting. I had to know.

My clammy hands lost their grip on the chair back. I wiped them on my top and climbed up again to the window. Hoping shadows covering my side of the building and grime on the pane would hide me, I peeked outside.

Two men in running tights, baggy shorts, and camo vests were bobbing their heads as a tall, brawny man facing away from me shook his fist at them. Wearing a baseball cap, T-shirt, and shorts, he slapped his sides and pointed in my direction. As he turned to face the building, his face made my heart sink into my gut—Falk—and I recognized the two men from the runners' group on Cedargrove. I decided this would not be a good time to scream for help. I could barely hear their voices through the window pane.

All three turned away from the building and walked back toward the alley. Their shouting grew fainter until an animal charging them caught their attention. A big animal, a lot like my Randy/dog, he slowed down and faced Falk and his men. I could hear his low growl and imagined him baring his fangs. I felt a surge of *schadenfreude. Hurray,* I thought. *Hope it scares the crap out of you, too.*

Falk patted his side for a weapon that was not on his hip. He yelled at one of the men, who then pulled a pistol-like piece from his vest. Falk grabbed it and aimed as the dog fled flat-out around the building. Falk fired electrodes, not bullets. No sound from the dog. I stifled a groan. He must have escaped.

One man—Carson?—yelled epithets for wasting his TASER. Falk, saying he thought it was a gun, dashed it to the ground. My mouth went dry. If Falk and his buddies thought the dog was a stray, they would shrug off the incident. If not, they would be coming for me, if only to move me elsewhere. Or would they? No matter. I had to prepare.

I slid off the chair and tried the door. Still locked. I rifled through the backpacks and found a rusty but sharp ball-bearing compass, good for stabbing. I flattened myself against the wall. As soon as Falk and company opened the door I'd dash outside. My kidnappers would be expecting me to be tied to the chair, half dead from dehydration. Let them think that.

Angry voices filled the lot. A car engine started up and drove away at high speed. From the sound of his cursing, I knew Falk was still there. Returning to the chair, I saw him kick the TASER's batteries.

From his shorts pocket he pulled out a cellphone and tapped his finger against the screen repeatedly. He must have reached someone's answering machine because it looked like he was having a one-sided chat. Chopping the air with his free hand, he finished and pocketed the phone again.

Never looking toward my window, Falk paced around the lot until a different car pulled in a while later. Bile burned my throat when I saw it was Pinscher's car, the one he parked near the trash burner the night Fanny/cat scratched him. He jumped out of the driver's side, slammed the door, and grabbed Falk by the arm. Falk shook him off and yelled "Didn't you want her?"

I swallowed the impulse to heave. Multiple sirens blared, muting Pinscher's answer, except for ". . . all wrong." A fire engine and several squad cars arrived, flying into the lot and discharging first responders including police. I rubbed away more of the window grime and saw a man's pant leg leaving the last car to charge into the lot, but Falk's screams grew louder, distracting me from seeing who it was.

Falk was pulling at his chin and wiping sweat off his brow as two officers with zip ties approached him. Raising his hands, Falk shouted, "No, wait, I'm an officer of the law. You're making a big mistake. Pinscher, tell them." Pinscher raised his hands as if to say he was helpless. Trotting backwards, Falk reached an ell of the building and hoisted himself onto a low wall. He leaped from there onto the lowest fire escape balcony and clambered up its ladders to the roof.

While the police officers were converging on him and urging Falk to surrender, Pinscher turned away and started toward my part of the building. I nearly kicked the chair over as I hopped to the door. In one hand I held my compass's sharp point, while I gripped my little flashlight in the other. I planned to stab an eye, whack his head, then run to the police.

The heavy bolt thudded as it dropped away from the lock holder. At the same time, a tortured wail rent the air. The door stayed shut. I tottered back to the window. On the far end of the roof, Falk was holding his head and blood was coursing down his chin. A cat jumped off his shoulder and leaped to the fire escape. She landed in the lot, and disappeared around the corner. A dog was attacking him, too. The dog's jaws gripped one of Falk's legs. Falk couldn't shake off the beast and staggered ever closer to the edge of the roof. In a flash the dog let go. The man lost his balance and fell to the ground.

The growing early dusk still allowed me to see the mess Falk made. A puddle of blood under his head oozed toward the rest of his twisted body. Pinscher reached him first, then a couple of EMTs approached. One of them felt for Falk's pulse and checked his breathing. The EMTs partner examined Falk's eyes, looked at Pinscher, then waved her hands as if to say, "That's it, folks." I ducked when Pinscher wiped his brow with a handkerchief from his back pocket and pointed to my window. While other officers were running toward the body with a gurney, I could hear Pinscher and a few other people approach my dungeon—or worse, my *crypt*, since I had been left to rot there.

An ambulance siren was wailing in the distance. Barely breathing, I pressed against the wall and waited. Pinscher's voice carried over the blare. "Careful, now. She may be in bad shape." As the door slid open, I leaped at Pinscher. "You piece of filth! Take this," I croaked and aimed the compass point at his head. A pair of hands stopped mine in mid-stroke and pulled it behind my back. I sloshed as much saliva as my dry mouth could summon and spit at my nemesis.

He stepped back. "Let me explain," he said, wiping his cheek with the back of his hand.

"Don't you dare touch me," I barked. Behind me, I heard, "Easy, Ella. You've got this all wrong." Dave's voice. I felt a gentle hand on my shoulder. He wound a light blanket around me. Arms immobilized, I dropped my weapons and stared open-mouthed at him. "You, too?" I asked. I had no saliva left to spit at him so, knocking Dave aside with my shoulder, I staggered out the door into the twilight.

No one stopped me. Out in the lot, a crew of EMTs were working on Falk's body. I heard one of them yell, "Up there! Naked man on the roof, calling for help." Two firemen ran to the ell with a pike pole and lowered the fire escape ladder from the first floor platform. One of them, wearing a backpack, climbed to the roof, vaulted the gooseneck rails at the top, and ran to the unclothed man curled over the parapet.

"Naked man?" I whispered. The sun had not quite set, but Randy had shape-shifted. The fireman looked him over, signaled a thumbs-up to his colleagues below, and wrapped a space blanket around him. We were a matched set, except I was still in my pajamas. Closing my eyes, I took in some deep breaths—inhale: one-two-three-four-five; exhale: one-two-three-four-five—and a bit calmer, I looked up.

Randy was returning my gaze. Worn and weary, yet he grinned and waved at me. Pulling a hand out of my wrappings, I waved back, then watched the EMTs pack up Falk's corpse and carry it away in the ambulance. Police officers were busy with all their crime scene activities. I turned wide-eyed to face three people next to me—my neighbors and Pinscher.

"Looks like that body has its rightful owner again," purred Fanny into my right ear. Dave stood on my other side. Pinscher hovered behind them. I recoiled. "Are you all in this together? Trapping me in that awful place?" I said, jutting my chin toward the deserted school. I was shaking non-stop.

Dave called over one of the cops. "Martin, we have to get her home and into a warm bed. Can you . . . ?" Without a word, the young man carried me easily to the last squad car. Fanny sat in the back with me. Dave sat up front. Pinscher hovered by the car. "I'll wrap things up here." Pointing to Randy descending the fire escape, he said, "That man. Ella, sorry, Mrs. Castle, is that—?"

"Don't—" I tasted bile and vomited the granola bar and a lot of stomach acid. Fortunately, the car door was still open, and I missed soiling the interior. That slug of water from the water bottle must have been really old.

"Not to worry, ma'am," the young officer assured me. A fireman ran over with some clean-up powder. Officer Martin offered me a bottle of water. I waved him off and flipped my hand to say he should leave. The police car soon lurched forward and spun out of the parking lot. In a minute or two, we were driving on Cedargrove.

Although my mouth was burning, I turned to Fanny and asked, "Were you . . .?" She put a finger to her lips and hissed in a whisper, "I just arrived. Only Falk knew that was your cat and he won't say a word." She scratched her nose with a pointed, blue fingernail and turned away to look out the car window. "Here we are, sergeant," she said. "We can take care of Ms. Castle now."

He parked the car in front of our building and hurried to open my door. Fanny was by his side in a flash. I stepped out, but my legs buckled, and I nearly fell. Fanny put an arm around my shoulders, while Dave held me by the waist. They steered me to the front door and both of them helped me up the stairs to my apartment.

Lonnie was waiting at my door. "Mr. Straybill called me, asked me to open since you probably didn't have a key." I nearly collapsed on the threshold, but Lonnie picked me up as if I weighed much less than my 135 pounds and settled me into my armchair.

Fanny shooed Dave and Lonnie out, saying she'd call when I was clean and rested. After a few futile objections they left, and Fanny went into the kitchen. "You need some quick liquid energy. I'll warm up some broth. Where do you keep it?"

"Look under the . . ." I pushed against the chair's arms but fell back, legs limp as plastic wrap. I couldn't lift my heavy head from the soft chair. I felt the warmth of a sweet-smelling cover, muttered "thanks," and crashed.

$$\sim$$

When I woke up, the room was dark except for my reading lamp next to the chair. A cat was curled at my feet. Shivering after a deep sleep, I recalled a vivid dream: Pinscher and I were at Caitlin's, but we were laughing at each other's jokes and toasting each other with champagne. "Hi, Fanny," I said to the cat. A light went on in my bedroom and another Fanny emerged, wrapped in her robe.

"Hi, there. Feeling better? Oh, her. She's just a little stray I'm fostering. I brought her here to keep you company." She hugged the gray cat and cuddled nose to nose. "Say hello to Ella, Felice." She plunked the cat onto a fluffy pillow bed, also installed in my living/dining room. "You could use a faithful companion, you know," she said. She waved her hands as if to clear the air. "But you need a shower more. Can I help you up?"

"But . . . that cat . . . she's just like—"

"Like the one attacking your foes?"

"Yes, that one. I thought she was you, since you told me you're a, what's it called . . . a shifter."

"I said that?"

"Fanny . . ." I must have looked ready to throw a punch.

Fanny laughed and whispered, "I am, I am, but this little one helps me keep my secret." She thrust Felice in my arms and my maternal instincts took over.

Cooing, I said, "What other secrets are hiding around here, kitty?" I wanted an explanation of all I'd been through, the series of bizarre and unnerving events punctuated by Falk's horrible accident and Randy's transformation on the roof. Fanny, too, was an unbelievable character, yet I needed to trust her. She had helped Lonnie protect his dad. I blurted, "Where's Randy? Is he safe?"

"I'll find out. Here, let me help you up. Your robe is in the bathroom. Can you make it on your own?"

"Sure, sure. Thanks, Fanny," I said as I handed Felice to her and shuffled across the room. My torn and stinky pajamas went in the garbage can, and I stepped into the shower. Grateful for the grab bars

I had installed, I held on and basked in a warm cascade of water. My skin burned from rubbing with a soapy washcloth. Worried about my cut knee, I rested my foot on the side of the tub and was about to wash my wound when I saw that it had closed. No sign of infection. That was fast, as quick a healing as Dave's head wound.

A layer of steam hid my reflection when I glanced in the mirror afterward, and I was grateful for that, too. Out in that parking lot, I must have resembled a Gorgon in a burrito to all those first responders. Hair combed, clean underwear in place, and wrapped in my soft chenille robe, I straightened my spine and returned to the living room. Fanny was teasing the cat with a length of yarn. She looked up while I was folding the blanket I now recognized as my mom's crocheted afghan. My chair was filthy from my jammies and prison dirt. When I finished cleaning the seat, Fanny asked, "Ready for broth now?"

"No, you sit, Fanny. I feel much better now, just not very hungry. Would you like a beer?"

Fanny walked to the window and looked out at the street. "I wonder if they nabbed those two runners." She turned to stare at me without a blink. "Not beer, thanks. Maybe mint tea or water?"

"Mint tea." As I filled the electric kettle, I asked, "You said runners. You mean the guys who ran by on Cedargrove with Falk?"

She sat on the couch and, legs coiled under her, sank into the cushions. "The same, also known as the men who kidnapped you last night. Since they bungled your restraints, they might not be the cold-hearted murderers of trash burner fame."

Of course. I mentally slapped my forehead. "I thought they looked familiar when I saw them with Falk in the parking lot. Are they part of your scheme?"

"My scheme?" Fanny's eyes widened.

"To make me feel crazy."

"Not us, but Falk and some of his running group, yes, they were after you. We have been building a case against Falk, but we'll never get a confession now." The corners of her mouth curled up. Licking at her tea, she said, "We never expected you to move here, of all places. Lonnie told me who you were, and I did all I could to protect you from Falk."

"Is Pinscher part of your 'we'?"

"Oh, him. You'll soon see who he is, really."

"But he's been Falk's buddy all this time. Why was he—"

Fanny was already at the door. "Ella, stop. You need to rest. I put a litter pan for Felice in your guest bathroom and kibble and water in the kitchen. Both of you need to nap. Oh, please attach the chain lock. Sleep tight." And she left, pulling the door until the handle lock clicked.

A chain lock? Who installed that? Not I, but I set it.

Felice lay curled in her pillow bed. I knelt on the floor. "So, Felice, I know it's early but I'm going to bed for a really long nap. I'll leave the door open for you if you need me. G'night." She flicked an ear and pursued her dreams. After putting on a boring night-shirt, I stretched on top of my covers and didn't wake up until the next day.

~

Loud knocking startled me awake and jump-started Felice in one bound from the bed and into the bath-room. "Mom, Mom, are you okay?"

Lonnie, asking me that asinine question again. "Yes, yes, I'm fine, but you scared the cat."

"We wanted to check on you, but there's a chain lock . . . did you say 'cat'?"

I slipped on my robe, pulled my hair into a velvet scrunchie, and, followed by Felice of the upright tail, undid the chain. "Hang on, I'm coming."

Lonnie leaned in to kiss my cheek while Dave and Pinscher remained on the threshold. When did Lon-nie blow his cover? He called me Mom in front of the two detectives. "What's *he* doing here?" I said, jutting my chin at Pinscher.

"Ella, please meet Detective Doug Pinsell. He has been on this case, too. May we come in?" Dave's faint smile weakened my resolve to excoriate him and ev-eryone else involved in this plot, especially for bring-ing along Pinscher/Pinsell to my home. Although I was sans makeup, sans nice clothes, and sans fresh breath, and scowling, I invited them in with a grand sweep of my hand. Although they all had suffered miserable me earlier, I was hoping they thought my appearance had improved with some sleep. Dave was holding two bottles and a few plastic champagne flutes.

"I brought some Bellinis from T.J.'s."

"What are we celebrating?" I asked as if I didn't know. "No partying until you all tell me what is going on. Sit down and start with the naked man."

Dave strolled into my kitchen and stowed his bottles in my refrigerator. Joining Pinsell and Lonnie on the couch, he said, "Ella, please, you sit, too."

I fiddled with the radiator valves and rubbed my upper arms. "It's cold in here today. Do you feel the chill?" No one answered. Lonnie squirmed. Nodding, Dave gestured toward my armchair. I sat and waited for them to begin. "Who's going first?"

"I'll fill you in on the man. Name's Randy Volkman," said Dave. "He's in the hospital and resting after some tests. We still don't understand why he was on the roof or where that dog and cat went. When I arrived at the hospital to check on him, Joe met me at the nurses' station by chance."

Lonnie interrupted, saying that Dave had seemed surprised to see him until he explained he was caring for the guy. "He has been living at my place all this time. Anyway, Mom—"

Dave shouted, "Mom? You called her Mom." His voice roughened. "I knew you were Ella Volkman, but . . ."

I studied Dave's reddening face. His eyes widened as he looked quickly from Lonnie to me and back again. "Explain," he said, "now that I see you three are one happy family."

"We've all been undercover, haven't we, Dave? Except Falk, really. He was the perfect villain."

"Ella, I need to explain. You know I suspected Falk's involvement in acquiring those Pine Glen properties and possibly those trash burner homicides." Dave stood up and paced around the living room. He looked out the window then came back to stand behind Pinsell.

"The only puzzle is why Falk had those people murdered. Making it look like the work of a mad dog but forgetting to leave clues that would mislead us. Who would know better than the Animal Control officer about how a dangerous dog on the loose could hurt someone? So, someone else handled it for him, and badly."

I said, "Falk acted so surprised when he discovered the body in the incinerator that rainy morning after I confronted Ra—sorry, the big, angry dog I saw lurking around that lot."

"*Acted* is the right word. It was such an easy set-up. You called about a threatening dog. The next morning there's an apparently dog-mangled body in the trash burner. I did question Joe when I reopened this case. I thought, he's the handyman, he'll know about the owners, whoever was paying him." Lonnie was staring at the floor, his hands clasped before him an inch or two above the rug. "I don't blame him for telling you not to trust me. And I didn't want Falk to suspect you were involved, but Falk was beginning to smell a rat."

Lonnie looked up from studying the floor. "Which is funny since he was in charge of Animal Control. Falk was a dangerous guy, and I was going crazy, trying to keep my mother safe. I also thought Pinscher was a crooked cop."

I finally closed my mouth and looked at Lonnie. I must have resembled a startled owl because Lonnie leaned toward my chair and patted me on my knee. Dave left the window and paced a bit before sitting next to Lonnie on the couch.

I gave Pinsell a death stare. "You were tailing me all this time?"

He started, "You know that—"

I cut him off. "What I knew was fear and loathing." I scanned the trio. "When will Randy Volkman leave the hospital?"

"He has no memory of living on Pine Glen. He has some kind of amnesia," Lonnie said with a nervous glance at Dave. "The police are out looking for that dog, but the animal left no tracks."

"My team has no leads so far. It's probably hiding. We'll straighten all this out soon. By the way, Evan Ferguson also suspected Falk's involvement. Doug here tried to keep him from pursuing the case. It wasn't his business, but the murders really bothered Evan, and he would have shared with me what he learned from you and forensics. Someone killed him, murdered him to shut him down." Dave clenched his jaw and took a deep breath. He pulled out his revolver, stretched past Lonnie, and aimed at Pinsell's head. "And that was you, Doug. Don't you dare move. Joe, or whoever you are, tie his hands."

Pinsell ducked. Shouldering Lonnie and Dave to the floor, he jumped up and edged toward the door. Dave stepped over Lonnie, but when he pointed his gun at Pinsell, a cat jumped on Dave's head. She shredded his scalp. Dave screamed and dropped his gun.

Felice leaped from him to the table. I scooped her up and backed away into the kitchen. Opening a drawer, I eyed my knives, but soon the tumult in the living room died away. Felice wriggled out of my arms and ran to Fanny, who somehow had entered my apartment and was cleaning up blood from the floor.

Dave's hands were bound behind his back. Pinsell was inserting Dave's gun into a plastic bag. "Dave, I've read you your rights, so I advise silence. Mrs. Castle, I should tell you this former Officer Straybill—actually, David R. Wright—was allegedly Falk's hidden partner, not I."

"Not Dave. No, I can't believe this. He's been trying to help me all this time. You," I said, jabbing my finger at Pinsell. "You were making me miserable."

Dave shouted as a police officer was steering him out the door. "Don't you believe him, Ella. I am your friend and wouldn't want you hurt, not ever." I heard him calling me as they went downstairs and out the door. "I'm innocent, Ella. You'll see."

Pinsell closed the door. "All this time, it appears Wright had been trying to find the owner or owners of the Pine Glen properties, plus this one. He, or they, hoped to have the city condemn all or most of the properties, including the trash burner and the school. Crazy, right? Ever since he served his sentence for manslaughter, he's been looking for a way to make a killing—so to speak."

"I don't understand. Are you saying that Dave Straybill, or whatshisname, Wright, is a murderer? Living right downstairs from me? I thought you, Officer Pinscher, led the gang." I collapsed into my armchair.

Pinsell cleared his throat. "I had nothing to do with the murders, as nasty as I appeared to be. Dave was right; I have been working undercover to solve this case. I played my part well, I see."

Too well.

Pinsell paced a bit before sitting next to Lonnie on the couch, while Fanny, quieter than usual, was watching us all. "There's more," he said, rubbing the back of his head.

"Like who was after Randy?" The unasked question was who had cursed him.

I turned to Fanny. What funny business had she been up to? "Do you remember my buying that chain lock for the door?"

"You didn't."

"That's right. I never bought one, yet there it is."

"Must have been a kind-hearted cat burglar who donated it."

"The same who 'infected' Randy?"

"No, Ella, Randy's illness had mysterious origins. That's all I can say right now."

I groaned, then asked her why, if she suspected Dave was dishonest, did she take care of his wound the morning we found him lying in the bushes? "Because you seemed to dislike him and his dog."

"I still don't like dogs in general—just my thing," she said with a glance at Pinsell. "Though I can say that King is one of the better sorts and I found a forever home for him. Anyway, Dave's wound was a fake—superficial, and probably self-inflicted. That's why he didn't want to go to the ER."

"Why would he do that to himself?"

"He got your sympathy, didn't he? And you had a chance to ask him about himself. Then he could lie to you about his so-called police work and the 'case' so he could discover the owner of the properties he and Falk wanted."

Pinsell broke in. "By the way, Evan Ferguson was Wright's—er, Dave's—friend, no lie, but not recently, as far as I could tell. Maybe Ferguson didn't know Wright was in the area or that he'd changed his name. Evan didn't know I'd been watching Dave. He never knew my real identity either, or he thought I was a crooked cop. I did have access to Evan's computer files. He had information about the trash burner murder victims in one. He probably intended to share it with the state's attorney, only someone murdered him before he could."

"Someone? Carson or Price?"

"Those mutts? No. They were in a police officers' running group that Falk took over. The guys complained he was a bully and most of them dropped out. Carson and Price stayed because he was blackmailing them about their puppy mill side business."

I stopped twisting my raw fingers and picked up Felice, who was playing with Pinsell's shoe laces. "Your shoes are untied. So, who killed Evan and why?"

Fanny went into the kitchen, took a glass, filled it from the faucet, and sat next to Lonnie on the couch. "Dave somehow knew Evan had information that would incriminate him, right, Pinsell? Ella, do you remember following me—shoot, I mean that feral cat—to the trash burner that night of the murder? You had no idea that Ferguson's corpse would be there, and Dave wasn't going to let you discover it without him."

"Dave?"

"Allegedly."

"But he was horrified when we found the body. He swore so much and vomited, I thought he would faint. Whoever would have connected him with the murder?"

"Exactly. Talk about gaslighting. Your real friends were keeping watch over you—in a way," she said, staring at the detective with her intense blue eyes. "We never meant you harm."

When I raised my eyebrows, Pinsell sat in the armchair and leaned back. "Now I need to know more about Randy Volkman, these properties, and his connection to the murders, while we have David Wright in custody for Evan Ferguson's murder."

Rubbing his arms, Lonnie said, "It's cold in here. Did you turn on the heat?" He patted the baseboard radiator and muttered, "It's on, barely." Then, turning to Pinsell, he said, "What happened to Ferguson's body? An ambulance took it away the night Mom and Wright found his corpse in the trash burner."

Pinsell wiped his face with a handkerchief and said, "Carson and Price had to act on the up and up. We collected whatever evidence we could at the site, took Evan's body to the morgue, filed our findings. We're still processing the stuff but Wright's DNA . . ." He paused, took a deep breath, and stood. "Look, I've talked too much already. Here's what I know: Wright allegedly killed Ferguson. Who killed the lawyer? We may never know, especially now that Falk is dead. Carson and Price might have some answers for us. Nothing certain at the moment."

"That's it?"

"Yes, Mrs. Castle. But Randy Volkman is also a person of interest."

"What? That's nuts. He doesn't even remember where he was when he was missing. Isn't that so, son?" By now Lonnie was standing by the window and watching the street.

"Right, Mom. He couldn't have been involved in any of that," he said with his back to us.

Fanny jumped up and stood in front of Pinsell, her eyes boring into his skull. "I'll have you know that Mr. Volkman was under my care these past few years. He was suffering from amnesia and a wasting disease that his doctors could not identify nor treat. His records are available and verifiable. I am a nurse practitioner and qualified to attest to his incapacities. You do understand, don't you?"

Pinsell sat stone-still, staring at her, his mouth agape.

"Answer me, Pinsell."

The detective blinked and said, "Mr. Volkman couldn't possibly be a suspect. Thank you for clarifying the situation."

Lonnie and I looked at each other and released a quiet, collective sigh. I nestled Felice in her kitty princess bed and said, "Folks, if you'll excuse me, I'd like to dress."

"You'd better change into street clothes right now," Lonnie said. "Look who's coming up the walkway."

I hurried to his side and saw a parked ambulance, lights off. Randy was wearing a jeans jacket and pants to match. A male nurse was guiding him toward the entry with one arm around his shoulders. Randy stopped, looked up, and waved to us. A smile snuck across my face, and I turned back to the others.

Pinsell stood, shook my hand, and thanked me for my cooperation, with the caveat that he might contact me later about my abduction and the prosecution of Carson and Price. "In the meantime," he said. "I hope you and your son will relax now that we have a case against Wright."

"From your lips to the ear of the cosmos," Fanny intoned as I waved goodbye and went into my bedroom. She must have let herself and Pinsell out while I was dressing, because the apartment was empty except for Felice when I came out, dressed in my cutest black leggings and artsy tunic. "Randy, Lonnie, are you still here?" I called out, hoping they weren't.

The second bedroom door creaked opened, and they peeked out. Randy was the first to speak. "It's daylight and I did not shift. Incredible, right? Can you stand me like this full time?"

"That depends. Do you have fleas?"

Settling onto the couch, Randy laughed and said, "Sometimes, I do get an itch . . . like, to stay with you . . . for the night."

Hoping my gulp was silent, I asked, "Coffee, anyone? I need some breakfast." I wasn't ready to talk about being a family again. Not yet. Fussing in the kitchen, I defrosted some blueberry scones and brewed coffee. No one spoke until I lay the breakfast tray on the table. "Oops, I forgot. Milk and/or sugar?"

Heads shook no. Lonnie cleared his throat. "Thanks, Mom, this looks great." He ate one scone in two bites and waggled his head toward Randy. "Dad wanted to share an idea with you."

"Yes. You see, Ella, with time on my hands, I thought a lot about what to do with the Pine Glen properties. The neighborhood might attract families if it had new, affordable multi-unit housing. Not high-rises but three-flats, six-flats, condos, and rentals. Not studios either, but units suitable for families."

Licking my scone's vanilla glaze, I asked, "You had time on your hands. Did you use it to think about me?"

"Lonnie benefits from the land trust, and, of course, I thought about you. Lonnie kept up with your news, except no one expected you to move into the Cedargrove unit."

"Dad knew you were here, even spied on you from next door," Lonnie said, rubbing his arms.

"Still cold?"

"No, Mom, just nervous."

"Our capital has grown, Ella," Randy went on. "Additional financing should be easy. We could apply for public funds, too. We talked about this, didn't we, Lonnie? Having a business again and a normal life, if ever?" He jumped up from the couch with arms spread wide to hug me.

I sidled away. My hands were strangling each other again. "No more talk right now about your real estate dreams. Your idea of a normal life has hardly matched mine, even before the curse altered our lives. We need time to think—about where to go from here, about what we want and need from each other, if anything. Go back to the cottage. I'm going to clean up here and do some of that thinking by myself."

Randy grabbed both my arms. "But this is about our life—all of us. You know what I've been through. Look, I'm totally human again and ready to start over. At least, let me stay here tonight and talk it over with you."

I wriggled out of his grip. Picking up our mugs and plates, I carried them to the sink and ran water over them. "Listen, I'm not ready for that. Not at all. Too many loose ends. Too many questions unanswered. Like, I understand how a money-hungry developer would try to force you into selling with a curse. But why didn't you trust me enough to tell me you were alive?"

Randy scratched the back of his head and looked at Lonnie, who shrugged, palms up, then said, "I think the curse came from one source, which Fanny found and changed, but who sent it? Falk was cunning and dishonest, but I don't think he ever practiced the dark arts. And Wright, I don't think he knew Dad was still alive. So, if not Wright or Falk the bully, then who?" Lonnie rubbed his temples and Randy plopped down on the couch again.

I almost dropped the plate I was rinsing. "'Bully' is not strong enough for him. How about malicious, unscrupulous, malign, arrogant—"

"Okay, Mom, I get it. We may never know who cursed Dad, but I think it won't happen again. The interested parties are out of the picture."

"Maybe. Falk's dead but there's no guarantee someone else isn't out there—someone involved in this scheme whom we don't know—preparing worse for Randy now that he's out of hiding." I picked up their jackets and walked them to the door. "I prefer spending time by myself, thank you. Please, go back to Pine Glen. I can't do this anymore today."

Randy grabbed the edge of the door and said, "Can we come back tomorrow, say around noon? We could text you before we leave."

"Fine, fine. Please, go. For now." I shut the door after them and attached the chain lock.

Finally alone, I relished the amber glow bathing my apartment, a soft cushion of light that settled over this town before the gloom of winter captured it. I needed to take a walk, and this would be the perfect hour to get outside myself and into the greater world.

I slipped on a quilted black jacket, tucked my gloves into a pocket just in case, then remembered Felice, still asleep in her princess bed. Freshening her water bowl and adding kibble to her feeder, I stroked her little velvet head and left for the street.

A soft cool breeze tickled my face. Zipping up my jacket, I set out in the direction of Marino's, not that I intended to shop. I wanted to leave this neighborhood for a while, forget what I'd seen and felt in a part of the city I'd mistaken as my perfect little village. Passing the supermarket, I wandered into blocks of new townhouses alternating with mid-rise apartment buildings. Retail and service businesses filled the ground floors: dry cleaners, nail salons, ATM machines in otherwise featureless spaces, a coffee shop, two lots with garden supplies. It all looked so peaceful. Uncomplicated.

My solo peace-quest ended abruptly. Fanny was by my side. Dressed in jeans, ankle boots, and a long gray coat, she kept pace with me without speaking. Her kindness and attention had rescued me many times, and I was grateful, but I did not feel like talking to her, or anyone, at that moment and resented the intrusion. We walked for blocks in silence until we reached a park with trails cutting across a meadow. Stopping by a small pond, I turned to Fanny and asked, "Why are you here? I'm sure you know I need alone time right now."

She pointed to a bench and said, "Because we have to talk. Let's sit, to make it easier on both of us."

"What will be *easier*?"

"My story. The part you haven't heard."

My cheeks burned and I felt a hot flash begin with its customary pit drop in my gut. As Fanny cleared her throat and wiped her mouth with the back of her hand, I felt sweat bathing my chest. "Fanny, I've heard enough by now. If it's about Dave, you don't have to explain. I understand."

"It's not about Dave, not directly." I'd never seen Fanny look uncomfortable and nervous before, not that way. She was wheezing and licking her coat's shoulder, her hands pawing at the zipper.

"What's going on? Do you know you look like an anxious cat?"

"Well, yes." She slapped her thighs. "I'm stopping an involuntary shift. Happens when I'm upset. Give me a few minutes"—she gasped— "to fix this. Then we'll talk." She pulled her knees to her chest. Her ankle boots were blue leather, both vamps etched with a cat head. Her long nails dug into her thighs and she rocked back and forth. Tucking her head into her chest, she muttered strange syllables, puffed a few times, then sat up again, a smile softening her face. "I'm better now. How are you?"

"Totally mystified but all ears. Are you sure you're okay?"

"Yes, quite sure. Are you ready to listen with no interruptions?"

I nodded, my heart approaching arrhythmia.

Fanny took a deep breath and began. "As you might have noticed, Falk and I were not strangers. Around the time of Cedric Rothman's murder, I was sniffing around the trash burner, in my human form. Thinking I could sense the situation better as a cat, I began to shift. I assume Falk had been watching the crime scene and noticed me there. He caught me shifting and grabbed me. Threatened to take me to the pound unless I did something for him. Somehow he knew that he could control me if he caught me during the shift. I spoke to him—yes, I can do that as a cat—and agreed to do what he asked if he promised to never reveal my identity and to leave me alone after I granted his request."

"That must have been terrifying. And you trusted him? No wonder you detested him. So what did he want?"

She sat up straighter and looked around. "You might not like this, but yes, he kept his word because I told him I knew a few other spells he would not want to experience."

I dabbed my forehead with a tissue. "Go on."

"He took me—still in my cat guise—to his office. After giving me some time to shift back to me, Fanny, in his bathroom, he sat me, dressed in an enormous robe, in front of his desktop computer and said, 'You're a witch. I have an enemy. I want you to curse him. Can you send an untraceable curse on the internet?' I am adept in some modern dark arts, but I'd never hurt anyone with them—not until that day."

Now my sweat was cold. I shivered and looked at this woman, a neighbor I had trusted—once. "Fanny, you—"

"No interruptions?"

I shook my head.

"I asked the name and email address of his enemy. I didn't know the man, not then. Falk agreed I could take a few hours to do the job after he understood I had to search for my sources on the dark web, then apply the curse with great caution. One mistake would be disastrous, for him and the accursed.

"Falk sent Carson to my apartment. The guy was an expert burglar—he didn't take anything from my place, only some clothes for me to wear. I lose my clothes when I shift, you see."

"Ach, that explains how they entered my apartment and kidnapped me."

"Ella, I—"

"I know, I know. Sorry."

Fanny jumped up from the bench and circled it, her eyes darting around the area. "I thought I heard someone coming." After lifting her head, as if catching an unwelcome scent, she sat again, closer to me, and raised her hand as if to pat my arm but stopped short. "Sorry, I had to check. Our conversation is private."

I looked around, too. Her wariness made me nervous. She went on. "No, don't worry. I didn't see or hear anything." Her voice was soft and nearly monotone. "As I said, I did not know Falk's enemy. I invoked a wasting curse, which would weaken the victim's body and resolve, but not kill the poor guy. Falk did not know that. I added that if Falk died, the curse would end. He let me go after I sent the curse to the man's email. Falk warned me he would be watching me from then on. I, in turn, warned him not to go too far.

"As for Lonnie, he and I met before you moved in. I knew early on he was no handyman, from his hands, his manner, and the way he couldn't fix my leaking faucet. But I could not imagine why he hung around our building on that pretext.

"Late one night, I was in the inner lobby and I heard his voice up in 2A. He was on the phone, on speaker, talking to his father. Was saying, 'Don't worry, Dad. We'll find a way to beat this disease.'" After hearing more of the conversation, I thought the man's symptoms sounded a lot like the curse I had set up for Falk. So, I marched upstairs and banged on the door of 2A. Joe—how I knew him then—took a while to open the door. I yelled at him for trespassing and making so much noise. He stammered a bit, then asked me to come in. Shutting the door, he said, 'Miss Katzer, I'm sorry. Let me explain. I was talking to my dad, who's dying from a disease his doctors can't cure, let alone identify. You won't believe this, but I think his computer is killing him. I don't know how to help him. It's sending strange signals.'

"I said there are many strange things in this world, so who knows, then asked him his father's name. Lonnie hesitated until I entered his thoughts and reassured him of my sympathy. He opened up and told me his story. My heart sank. At that moment, I knew the victim and I vowed to find an antidote, but I did not want Lonnie to suspect I was involved. So, I told him I felt sorry for him and hoped something would turn up that would help, but he couldn't use 2A anymore. Too risky. I did worry Straybill would hear him, too, and might suspect something. I warned Lonnie to be careful. He appeared grateful I believed him. We left 2A. He locked up and went out the back way."

"Can I ask a question? Please, Fanny?"

"Go on, as long as you don't yell at me."

"It sounds like you never trusted Dave. Why? I did, at times."

"The dog, King. I could tell Dave was not kind to him. If he was abusing King, I wanted to know. I listened outside his door. Instead, I heard Dave talking to someone about a scheme to get the Pine Glen properties. With some effort, I realized he was talking to Falk. That will never hold up in court, but it was enough to sour me on the man. Everything adds up today—his interest in you and Randy, his lies, his manipulations; but, funny thing, he never suspected Lonnie."

I sat there, nodding, rocking a little, but not looking at Fanny. She went on. "I created an avatar, connected to Randy's computer and you know the rest of the story."

I just stared at her. "And you knew who I was? Why didn't you help me?"

"I did, but in my way."

Of course, she did help. At the trash burner. In the alley with Pinscher. In my apartment. She had been watching over me from the day I moved in, all the while protecting Lonnie and Randy from Dave and anyone else who might harm them.

Fanny jumped up again, grabbed my arms, and yelled, "Run! This way." She was pulling me along the path leading to a bridge that spanned one end of the pond. "They're coming. I don't know how they—anyway, I'm calling for backup."

Out of breath, I couldn't run anymore once we reached the middle of the bridge. Behind us three men were crossing the meadow toward us. Fanny tore at her coat, jeans, boots, and the rest and handed them to me. Naked, she left the bridge. In a few moments she emerged from a thicket in her cat shape, surrounded by a crowd of cats—black, brown, calico, orange tabbies, and a few grays. She invaded my thoughts and ordered me to hide behind the thicket with her clothes.

Through prickly branches I spied on the cats. The men saw them, too, and hesitated at the other end of the bridge. Dry twig ends snapped in my angry fists. Carson, Price, and Pinsell—together. They looked at each other, none of them willing to cross the bridge. Pinsell pointed to the path circling the pond. Half the cats followed his gesture and ambled toward the path. The men looked in the other direction. So did a few of the other cats.

I heard a low growl behind me. The hair on the back of my neck bristled as a pack of dogs, an immense mastiff leading them, passed me and sat at the end of the bridge closest to Fanny. A German shepherd, an Aussie, a gray pit bull and—King!—were licking their jaws as they stared at Pinsell. I sensed Fanny's message: *My shifter friends.*

I answered her thoughts: *King, he's one, too?*

Pinsell stepped onto the bridge and, closer to the mastiff, pulled out a TASER from under his suit jacket. He aimed it at the huge dog but, before he could fire, cats from all directions leaped on the three men. Pinsell's gun fired. TASER prongs hit Price, the smallest of the three men. He fell backwards with a scream as the hit induced a seizure. Pinsell was fighting off the cats and Carson rolled on the ground with the pit bull, whose jaws were clamped around one of his arms.

Fanny spoke up. I expected a meow, but she said, "I'm going to shift now right here. Don't look." Soon, a clothed Fanny emerged and stood next to me. "We're safe. My friends are handling this." When I looked at the scene on the bridge, several men, including a policeman, were binding Pinsell's wrists and tending to Carson and Price's wounds. Imagine, a policeman shifter!? How many were living among us ordinary folks?

A young man with a light brown complexion and a halo of dark curly hair strolled toward us. Standing in front of me, he kissed my cheek and said, "I will never forget your kindness and those treats."

Before I could answer, he ran away. In the distance I could see him raise a triumphant fist in the air. King, free of Dave at last?

~

"Pinsell was doubly undercover. Falk and Wright believed he was partnering with them, but he had plans to cut them out and take it all for himself." Fanny and I were leaving the park after a stroll around the now peaceful pond path. All cats and dogs had left for their daytime jobs. "Your instincts about Pinscher or Pinsell—whichever—were dead-on," she said.

I stopped to sip the coffee I'd bought from a mobile vendor. I needed to digest all this information, and coffee would help. "But I thought you had bewitched Pinscher when the police arrested Dave. That you'd blocked him from investigating Randy." Fanny shook her head, and I realized that Dave and Pinscher had been equally adept at lying and manipulating me, and each other.

"How did all your shifter friends—and who knew that there were so many?—how did they know Pinscher was following us?"

"Instinct and a bit of telepathy. Cats and dogs not only have acute senses like smell and hearing. They also have strong intuitions. My friends sensed my distress and were there the first time my instincts hinted someone was following us."

"That's hard to believe. They came so quickly."

"True confessions. I did let a few of them know I was going to find you and explain stuff. They were on the alert."

"Like that mastiff?"

"Yes, Officer Martin." I must have scowled in confusion. "That nice, young officer who drove you home after the kidnapping."

"No wonder."

"No wonder what?"

"No wonder he was so helpful. That's all. So, Fanny, now what?"

We reached the end of our Cedargrove block, opposite Pine Glen Street. Fanny hadn't answered me, not since my question, but I was relieved to have some quiet to sort out my thoughts. In front of our building, furniture and a mattress were sitting in a pile by the curb. I recognized Dave's desk, its empty drawers gaping in the autumn chill. I shivered. "What a way to end, eh? I suppose he won't be out on bail."

"Not my business now. The machinery of law has taken over."

"With help from your friends."

"Right." She seemed to be looking through me as she said, "As for the future, I'm leaving." When I burst out with "Oh, no. You can't. Why?" and a half dozen other objections, she waved them away. "Ella, I need new territory. Cats are like that. Randy broke the curse all by himself—well, yes, as a shifter and with a little help. Lonnie is free now to live his dreams instead of a nightmare. And you—I know you will have a good life soon with them. You will not need me nor any of my feline fun. Besides, now you have Felice."

"But you've been my friend since I moved here, although I may not have appreciated your help at times. How will I manage without you?"

"Do you hear yourself? The woman who bolted from her kidnappers, who survived would-be killers, who bought herself a Trolley because she loved living here, shopping for herself, and having a cozy home?"

She let me hug her but ran into 1515 before I could say any more. I looked at the jumbled heap of Dave's belongings, then back at our building's façade. It was a nice place to live, good enough until Randy and I renovated the cottage to make it our home, a very right move.

KITCHEN MAGIC

(published by Cloaked Press, *Fall into Fantasy* 2017)

A T FIRST, THE WOMAN jangled her plastic cup in the air as if she were a holiday bell ringer. Then she caught Ellis Felcher's eye and smiled. Ellis was sure the woman would ask for a handout, but she pulled her sweater more tightly around herself and said "Getting colder, isn't it? Go home and make yourself some soup."

Ellis surprised herself by stuffing a dollar in the woman's cup. Muttering, "I can't cook," she nearly missed the woman's chirpy, "Oh, you will. You will! Thanks for talking to me." Ellis continued west on Division Street and passed her neighborhood drugstore. Under the canopy sheltering the store's entrance, a lean woman in a worn wool coat stepped aside as Ellis pushed the revolving door. "Hi. Just to let you know, there a sale on today."

"Sorry, what did you say?"

"They even have canned appetizers, like duck pâté. Thanks for talking to me," said the woman.

Ellis couldn't suppress a small smile. She nodded her thanks and went inside, thinking, *All these sad people. I feel sorry for them. She must be lonely. Probably will ask me for change later.* When Ellis left the store, the woman was gone. She shrugged, hefted her bag of purchases onto her hip, and trudged on home.

~

Ellis and her mother, Rena, quarreled a lot in the two-bedroom high-rise apartment they shared near Lake Michigan. Rena loved her view of the Chicago lake shore, bisected by a high-rise closer to the lake, which, as far as she was concerned, constituted a lake view. Ellis argued that life would be more interesting and the apartment less expensive, if they were closer to the street.

Rena was attached to familiar objects, like her collection of little Limoges boxes and her deceased husband Hal's armchair. She didn't notice the chair's scuffed legs and threadbare upholstery. Ellis prayed a new job—if it materialized—would let her move out of her mother's time capsule.

Rena warned her that time was passing; Ellis had no job and no dates. She didn't understand how her pretty, Phi Kappa Phi honors-awarded, twenty-five-year-old couldn't get work or find a boyfriend. "Don't waste your days sitting and reading." Rena jutted her chin toward a stack of books on the coffee table. "At least, send out a résumé."

"I have, Mom. You know they go unanswered. I've mailed and emailed more than a dozen. And don't start with the boyfriend thing. Your last fix-up . . . let's not talk about it." Ellis clutched a book to her chest and sank into her father's armchair.

"Well, stop reading so much and come in here." She beckoned Ellis into the kitchen. "Since you haven't found your ideal job yet, I'll teach you to cook a few good meals. The path to a man's heart . . ."

"Oh, Mom." Ellis' book landed on the carpet with a thud. "Please. I'm the worst cook."

"Not if you knew a few basics. C'mon." The doorbell squealed. "Who could that be? How did they get past the doorman?"

"Maybe it's a neighbor." Ellis picked up the novel she despaired of ever reading uninterrupted and went to the door. Looking through the peephole, she whispered to Rena, "I don't know him, but he looks . . . actually, ok." Before Rena could stop her, Ellis opened the door and said, "Hello, can I help you?" to a tall, handsome man dressed in an expensive-looking gray sweater. neat trousers, and nice shoes, like a pair she noticed recently in a Michigan Avenue store window.

"Hello, I'm Michael Magnus. My mom lives in the penthouse above your place."

Rena joined them at the door and rolled her eyes. "Ellis, don't make him stand out there in the cold. Come in, Michael. I'm Rena Felcher, my daughter Ellis. I met Cheryl, your mother, on the elevator today, as a matter of fact. We had a nice conversation. She told me a little about you, too, that you're in financials and graduated Phi Beta Kappa and—"

"Mom!"

"I'm sure she did," Michael smiled as he walked into the living room and looked around. "It's embarrassing, frankly. Anyway, that's why she sent me down, to you. She's desperate and she said you seemed so nice."

Rena's forehead puckered. "I am. Nice. What's wrong?"

Michael was smiling at Ellis, who was staring at her book's cover and stroking its spine. "Well, Mom remembered your saying what a terrific baker Ellis was."

"What?" Ellis blurted.

"Mom doesn't know the first thing about baking and was hoping Ellis might whip up some cookies for her meeting tonight. The people coming think Mom's a terrific home baker. The bakeries are closed now and convenience store cookies . . . well, you know."

"Ellis would be *delighted*. How much time do we have?"

Michael looked at his smartphone. "It's half past five. The meeting's at 8:30."

Rena flapped her hand down. "Pssh. No problem. Ellis will make two dozen, ok?"

Michael grabbed Ellis' hand and shook it vigorously. "Oh, thank you. You're making life a lot easier for me. See you later." Michael left and closed the door behind him.

Ellis stood looking at the door with mouth agape. "Mother, how could you?"

"Don't worry. I'll run out, get some chocolate chips and pecans. Oh, and butter. I'll bake them up in a jiffy."

"But, Mom . . ."

Rena was a whirlwind. She grabbed her purse and coat, opened the door, looked down the hallway, then dashed to the service elevator. Winking, she waved good-bye as the elevator door closed.

Several hours passed and Rena wasn't home yet. Ellis held her smartphone at a distance and moaned, "What are you saying, Mother, that there are no chocolate chips? Every store is out of them? That's crazy. Please, come home. We'll tell them the oven broke down." She froze at the sound of a soft knock on the door. "Oh, Mom. They're here. I'll think of something."

She pocketed her phone and went to the door. Through the peephole she saw not her handsome neighbor, but the soft face of an elderly woman wearing a shabby man's cardigan and a broad smile filled with healthy teeth. The woman waved. Feeling the heat of embarrassment flood her cheeks and neck, she recognized the panhandler from her walk home.

Ellis opened the door. "Hello?"

"Hi. Oh, my poor girl. Why so sad?"

"My upstairs neighbor expects me to bake chocolate chip cookies. I don't know how. My mom's not here and . . ." She thought, *why am I telling her this?*

"I know, I know. But would you invite me, Polly Pilgarlic, to your wedding with Michael if I bake the cookies for you?"

What wedding? What's she talking about? How does she know Michael? Ellis did want to have cookies ready for Michael now that her mother had put her on the spot. *What have I got to lose?* "Well, if you would bake them, I'd be . . . um . . . delighted to welcome you to . . . the wedding, Polly . . . er . . . Pilgrim?"

"Pilgarlic, dear. Thank you. Now, shoo. Kick off your shoes and sit right there in your father's chair while I bake."

Such a sweet face. Can I trust her? How did she know about my Dad's old chair? I suddenly feel so very tired. Ellis tucked herself into the chair and yawned. "OK, thanks, Polly." She stretched and pulled her mother's old afghan over her shoulders.

A firm knock at the door woke Ellis. She slipped on her flats and hurried to the kitchen. On the counter sat a beautiful tin box. A winter snowscape decorated its lid. Ellis could smell chocolate, a hint of vanilla, and loads of butter. She peeked under the lid and saw more than a dozen cookies, neatly stacked and glistening.

Michael called to her from the other side of the door. Ellis picked up the box and greeted Michael with a broad smile. "Hello. I think you'll like these."

Taking in the enticing scent of cookies, Michael lifted the lid. "These look delicious! Thank you. I know Mom will be grateful. By the way, she'd like both of you to come to her dinner party tomorrow night, that is, if you're free."

His description of the party hung in the air as Rena came off the elevator with a big bag of groceries in her arms. "There you are. Tell your mother we'll have the cookies ready in just a little while."

"You're funny, Mrs. Felcher. I have them here and thank you again. Ellis, tomorrow at 8:30?"

Ellis nodded.

"I'll come by for you then. 'Bye." Michael hugged the tin box and used the service stairs to return to his mother's penthouse.

Rena stared at her daughter. Ellis caught the groceries before they hit the floor.

"Come in, Mom. I took care of everything."

～

The next morning, Mrs. Magnus phoned. "Ellis, what a hit those cookies were. They vanished in minutes. How *did* you do it?"

"Thank you. Just a secret family recipe," she coughed.

Rena was on the extension. "Cheryl, sorry. I couldn't help myself. Isn't my Ellis wonderful? She can cook anything."

"For example . . . ?"

"Um, what would your guests like?"

"Well . . . they are mad for duck pâté."

"Ellis makes that *all* the time."

"Could you make some for us tonight? My guests would be so impressed."

Ellis was desperate and shook her head, but Rena said: "Why not? Of course, Ellis will whip some up."

"Fantastic. I am impressed and so was Michael," she chuckled. "He likes you, Ellis. Mother's instinct."

Between the impossible task of whipping up a gourmet pâté and the heart-quickening thought that Michael Magnus was interested in her, Ellis could hardly speak. "Mrs. Magnus, I . . ."

"She'd be delighted. We'll see you later," Rena trilled and hung up.

Ellis stood holding the receiver of her old princess phone, one of two touchtone devices left from the eighties that Rena clung to. *What now? Mrs. Magnus—and Michael—will see I'm a fraud. They think I'm a gourmet cook and wouldn't even care that I have a graduate degree in comparative literatures.*

Her coat halfway on and her purse flying behind her, Rena burst into Ellis' room. "I don't know how you managed to bake those cookies yesterday, but I'm going to make the pâté. Don't you worry. See you soon." Once more, she flew out the door and left via the service elevator.

"Now, what am I going to do? Mom will never find the ingredients in our neighborhood." She sank into her father's chair again and stared out the window. "C'mon. Ellis. Don't be so upset, just because you wish you were at work now and none of this had happened." She covered her eyes with her palm, shook her head, and groaned.

She lifted her head at the sound of a soft knock on the door. Rappity-rap-rap. Ellis looked at the door. Rappity-rap-rap. She leaped out of the chair and ran to the peephole. Standing opposite her was that lean, older woman from the drugstore, dressed in her clean, but tatty tweed coat. She was carrying a bulging cloth sack. Spying Ellis' eye in the peephole, the woman waved and said, "I am Patricia Pollywog and I am here with duck liver pâté if . . ."

Ellis yanked open the door and pulled the woman inside. "If?"

"How do you do?"

"Not so well, thank you. And you were saying?"

"Ah, yes—*if* you would be kind enough to invite me to your wedding to Michael Magnus."

Not again. Marrying me is not on Michael's agenda. I'm sure he'd just like to go out or something. But she does look kind and I feel so wiped out by all this. Miss Pollywog?"

"*Mrs.* Pollywog."

"Mrs. Pollywog, if you provide the duck pâté, you would be a most welcome guest at my wedding."

"Then, consider it done. You look tired, dear woman. Change your clothes for the party and rest until Michael comes for you this evening." Ellis was about to object, saying her mother was out shopping and would be back soon.

"I'll make sure Rena Felcher is happy. Don't you worry. Now, scoot."

Ellis thought, *how does she know Mom's name?* Mrs. Pollywog's coat lay neatly folded across the back of Dad's chair. Wearing a patchworked apron, the woman stood in the kitchen, her chin in one hand. "I said, scoot. When you're dressed, you'll find the pâté in the frige." Ellis gave her a bewildered look, went into her bedroom, and closed the door.

∼

When Michael first knocked on the front door, Ellis barely heard him. Rena rustled into her room, dressed in her satiny, flounced cocktail dress from the vintage shop. "Honey, wake up. Michael is here. I had the strangest dream, by the way."

"I'll bet you did."

"Yes, this lovely lady in an amazing, sparkly evening dress was singing the most beautiful song to me and—"

"Michael's still knocking, Mom. Where's my comb? Please help me find my dress."

"You're wearing it."

"Oh, right. Mrs. Pollywog said . . ."

"Mrs. who?"

"Oh, never mind. Just answer the door, please. I'll be there in a minute."

"Of course, and I have the perfect excuse for not bringing the pâté."

"What? Isn't it in the frige?"

"In the frige?"

"Again, never mind. Please let Michael in."

Rena went to the front door and opened it with a curtsy to Michael. Ellis went to the refrigerator and found a white porcelain casserole covered with plastic wrap and filled with pâté. She carried it to the front door and handed it to Michael.

Rena's mouth was hanging open. "Mother," Ellis whispered, "smile."

Rena regained her composure and said, "We'll just be a minute." She retrieved her house keys and shoved them into a minaudiere. She turned the clutch over and over in her hands. "Where did this come from?" she croaked to Ellis."

"Same as the cookies," Ellis winked. "Shall we go?"

Michael was marveling about the pâté. "This is amazing. Are you a professional, Ellis?"

"No, not at all. I do editing and translations," she coughed, "and I'm currently between jobs."

"And you found time to do this." Michael paused and looked at her intently. "Where did you apply for a job?"

"Knapher Press, for one."

Rena pushed them out the door and locked up. "Enough small talk. Ellis is amazing. One in a million, Michael."

They went up the elevator to the penthouse.

~

The party was wonderful. Everyone loved Ellis's pâté. The music was danceable and the conversations lively. At the end of the evening, Michael asked Ellis if she'd like to spend more time together.

Over the next few weeks, they explored the city parks and gardens, strolled along the lakeshore, and snacked on Chicago's many different ethnic foods. Michael never failed to note that none of the cafes or shops could match her cooking.

Ellis wished she could tell Michael about Polly and Patricia, but whenever he brought up her cooking, she changed the subject to his work or her studies and experience editing. She thought, *he'll think I've lost my mind if I say anything about those women.*

Two months passed. Michael and Ellis realized they were in love. Michael proposed, Ellis accepted, and they set the wedding date. Mrs. Magnus insisted on arranging the festivities at her club, the Casbah, and she wouldn't hear of Rena's paying for anything.

The wedding day arrived. Mrs. Magnus and Rena chatted with the guests and talked about how lucky

Michael was to have such a good cook for a wife. Ellis didn't care much for those conversations, but before she could change the subject, the club porter came up to them and said to Ellis, "Miss Ellis, your godmother, Polly Pilgarlic, asks if she might enter. Her name is not on the guest list."

"Polly who?" Rena stage whispered.

Ellis blushed, but Michael said, "Ellis, did you invite a Mrs. Pilgarlic?" When she nodded, he told the porter, "Tell Mrs. Pilgarlic that she is quite welcome."

The porter turned away and soon the little woman floated into the room. Dressed in her baggy sweater, she shook everyone's hand. When the porter offered to hang her sweater in the club's coat check, everyone gaped at the beautiful couture sheath Polly's sweater was hiding.

Mrs. Magnus could not help staring. Realizing her gaffe, she shifted her gaze to Polly's smile and her teeth, so even and shining, despite the woman's advanced age. "How do you keep your teeth so beautiful? I have such trouble with mine. You must give me the name of your dentist."

"No dentist, my dear. I just stay away from sweets. Never touch them."

Michael chimed in: "I agree, Mother, Ellis and I should do the same. Do you agree, Ellis?"

Ellis nodded again.

"Anyway, sweets are fattening and Ellis won't have time to bake with her new job at Knapher Press."

"Knapher, Michael? Did you say 'Knapher'?"

"Yes, I did. They were looking for an editor with your talents, so I mentioned you to someone I know there and—"

The porter interrupted them again. "So sorry, but another godmother, a Mrs. Patricia Pollywog has arrived and she is not on the guest list either."

"Patricia Pollywog?" Rena blurted.

"You *remember* her, don't you, Mom? Our dear, *dear* family friend," Ellis said, glaring at Rena.

Michael repeated the welcoming message and the porter escorted Mrs. Pollywog to them.

"How nice to meet you, Mrs. Pollywog," Cheryl said, with a raised eyebrow at the sight of Patricia's coat. "Please let the porter put your coat in the checkroom." The porter left with the coat after giving an appreciative glance at the woman's bronze sequined gown.

Cheryl had a coughing fit. Recovering, she asked, "How do you maintain such a svelte figure, Mrs. Pollywog? I have struggled with my weight for years."

Patricia looked Cheryl up and down. "Dear Mrs. Magnus, I never, ever, touch duck pâté. It would ruin my figure."

Michael interjected, "And since Ellis will be working with the chief editor of Knapher, don't expect her to whip up any more pâté, Mother." Michael beamed at his soon-to-be wife, locked arms with her, and bid the ladies good-bye until after the wedding.

Ellis treasured Michael's last words before the ceremony: "Dearest Ellis, I have a wedding day surprise for you. I've been studying at the Cordon Bleu. You won't have to lift a spoon or a pot in our kitchen unless you feel like cooking alongside me. Just say the word."

"I do and I will."

A Fairy Tale—The End

The Mole and the Rising Tide

(2022) A Poem

The mole having dug three tunnels
Sat in a hole within her burrow deep,
One tunnel led to the variable air.
Another to her nest of sleep.
The third untouched, a fearsome snare.
To the sea.

Alone she slept within her nest
Without old friends, by no decree.
All said she gave to them her best
But frowned as they sought the sea.
Without a care.

They left, they ran, into the sea
From ripe and narrow beds, they fled.
They screamed as water set them free
From holes they feared would keep them dead.
Not to be.

The mole dug more and built a dam.
In comfort she would live above
The waters dark that drowned her clan
And robbed her of the ones she loved.
Her tears ran deep.

Night would squeeze its paw around
Her as she curled within her lair.
A scrape and shuffle then unbound her
When another mole appeared to dare
Her to depart.

"The world is bigger than this hole and
Much more lies beyond the sea.
Come with me to see the land.
We two will start a dynasty."
She bit his nose.

The mole has dug another path.
Outside but hidden from the tide
She sits above the darkening sea
Where she can watch the otters glide.
And thinks of him.

"So right, so true were you, my love"
She sighed and scurried down below.
"I'll gnaw, and scrape through continents
Until I find you, sweet Hello."
And she left.